No One Has Any Intention of Building a Wall

Ruth Brandt

First published November 2021 by Fly on the Wall Press
Published in the UK by Fly on the Wall Press
56 High Lea Rd
New Mills
Derbyshire
SK22 3DP

www.flyonthewallpress.co.uk

Cover photo author's own. The cover photo shows a detail from a piece of street art found painted on a house in Jozefinska Street in the Podgorze area of Krakow which is mentioned in the story 'The Chair'.

Fly on the Wall Press is committed to the sustainable printing and shipping of their books.

MIX
Paper from
responsible sources
FSC® C022174

Supported using public funding by
ARTS COUNCIL ENGLAND
LOTTERY FUNDED

Dedicated to my family and friends for their love and encouragement, and to everyone who finds themselves on the outside.

Acknowledgements

Many thanks to all the individuals, publications and competitions who have encouraged, cajoled, and quite frankly told me to do better during my writing journey. Not least, Tim and Sylvia, my original writing buddies; tutors and fellow students on the Kingston University MFA programme, including Dr James Miller and Jonathan Barnes, and Mohamed, Jon and Mark; and all the wonderful writers in Betas and Bludgers, established by Matt Kendrick.

Without the hard work of so many individuals who run competitions and magazines, I would not have striven to raise the standard of my writing. So, many thanks to the organisations and publications who saw merit in my stories, including:

Happy Ever After, published in *Neon* Literary Magazine, Issue 40, Winter 2015 and nominated for the Pushcart Prize 2016 and Write Well Award 2016.

The Chair, published in *Brittle Star*, Issue 36, April 2015 and in *The London Reader*, Summer 2018.

Some Place to Eat, published in *Fictive Dreams,* July 2018.

Letters from Prague, published in *Litro*, March 2011 and the Aesthetica Creative Writing Anthology 2017.

Heading West, longlisted in the RA & Pin Drop Short Story Award 2017 (under the title of Going West).

A Contemplation of Rain and Ducks, placed 2nd in the Writers' Retreat Short, Short Story Competition 2020 and published online in April 2020.

Lifetime, highly commended in the Calderdale Short Story Competition 2009.

Voices, shortlisted in the Telegraph Short Story Club September 2012 competition.

Superstitions, published in *Litro* Issue 121, December 2012

Petrification, published in *Litro* Issue 141, May 2015

Strands, shortlisted in the Mslexia Short Story competition 2015.

Snow Blindness, published in *Gold Dust*, Summer 2013.

Tonight's Dream, runner up in the STORGY Short Story Competition 2013 and published by *STORGY*.

Shooting Waters, published by *Into The Void*, Issue 7, Quarter 1 2018 and nominated for Best Small Fictions 2019.

Stop All the Clocks, published in the Take Tea With Turning Anthology, 2012, and *The Broken City Magazine*, Issue 23, Winter 2018.

The Sundance Kid, published in the *Bandit Fiction* Winter 2017 pamphlet.

Lucky Underpants, highly commended in The Bridport Prize Flash Fiction competition 2018 and published in The Bridport Prize Anthology 2018.

No One Has Any Intention of Building A Wall, shortlisted in the Bristol Short Story Prize 2011 and published in the Bristol Short Story Prize Anthology Volume 4.

The collection, No One Has Any Intention of Building a Wall, won the Eyelands Book Award 2018 for an unpublished short story collection and longlisted in the International Beverly Prize 2019.

And finally, thank you to Isabelle and everyone at Fly On The Wall Press, not just for publishing my work, but for releasing challenging and exciting new writing into the world.

Contents

Happy Ever After

At the eight-hour mark Alfie's mother lies on his bed and pulls his pyjamas to her nose. She breathes in the scent of her son, little flakes of his skin which must still lurk there. She bundles up the fabric, squeezing every last atom of him into her, needing to capture any remaining fragments of his life so that she can nurture them within her again. Downstairs a kettle clicks on, or is it off? It doesn't matter. The room illuminates rhythmically blue. The front door slams. Boots paw the mat. A new voice. She wishes she had closed Alfie's bedroom door, shut them all out.

Josh Bubble Smith

wot the fucks happened wiv alf?

Like . Comment .

10 people like this

View all 6 comments

> **Chloe Spragg** sumfing happened?????
>
> Like
>
> **Matt Winterbottom** police round the park fuckin hell
>
> 2 people like this
>
> **Yasir Husseni** Whats up??!!
>
> Like

Between the twenty-fifth and fortieth day Alf is spotted disembarking from a vaporetta in Venice; cycling along Regent Walk in Edinburgh; and alighting from a metro train at Avtovo station, carrying a bottle of *Russian Standard* vodka and tapping ash off a *Belomorkanal*. His description is consistent: five foot eight (some an inch taller, some an inch shorter), dark woollen coat, bulbous hat, just as pictured in his photo. By the fiftieth day, the reports that have been pouring in from all over the place have begun to tail off.

Each sighting is definitely Alfie, his mother is certain of that. He loves travelling, he loves history and politics. *Remember, DI Potter, he is studying those at college.*

When DI Potter leaves, she shrinks into the sofa, imagining the chill of the St Petersburg November air, feeling the ache of lungs unaccustomed to smoke, clenching her gullet to prevent the wave of seasickness that consumes her.

On the third day, there are no sightings. Nor on the fourth.

On day minus seven, Alf sits in Lightwater Country Park with Eleni straddling his lap while she pokes her tongue into his ear. Her dribble tickles his neck and he laughs, smoothing his jeans-contained erection against her fanny. Perhaps they'll head into the copse where, from certain angles, there's a chance they might not be seen having sex. Or perhaps they will stumble back to his place and head up to his bedroom where his mum still insists on folding his clothes.

College has just started and he should be in a politics lesson, or is it travel and tourism? He doesn't remember anymore since he chose the subjects at random and hasn't downloaded his timetable, or looked at the book list, or actually ever turned up. A disappointment? Of course, but then Alf has contributed decent servings of disappointment to the world since the moment he broke free from his mother's womb; an ugly mass with a deformity that had failed to declare itself on scans.

"So much for fucking technology," his father had said in pretty much his last contribution to Alf's life other than a card sent on Alf's sixteenth birthday. If Alfred was ever in the Crewe area, he must drop in, it said. Otherwise, as Alfred had now passed from boyhood to manhood, his father guessed that was it. Go for it, son. Get in there.

Alf's first operation to reduce the spasms in his malformed leg failed. Never mind, eh; life would ultimately compensate the poor little mite in some way, after all, that's how it goes, isn't it?

His second operation was successful but it left Alf with a pause in his step, a hint of a limp which, by Year 3, turned Alf into the shark in the playground ocean, a basker who ate first and vomited up indigestible bones. Options? Eat or be beaten. Which was he to choose, Mother?

Since his disappointing GCSE results, Alf has spent his summer providing pools of neon-blue *WKD* vomit for the moonlight to glint off, far more poetic than barely-digested burger in vodka on the carpet. Used condoms under his bed should have contributed too, except Alf hasn't actually managed to get one out and on in his six-week sex fest with Eleni. Still, he has jammed the unopened pack of condoms down the side of his bed to prevent sex-squeak, where it loiters, waiting to fly out when his mother changes his sheets. Unused pack versus used condom? Either way his mother's disappointment is assuaged now that he has a girlfriend to keep him away from that lot. She's the icing on the cake, Eleni is, proof that her ugly duckling has matured into a cob. Her boy is finally on the road to coming good.

Alf would have liked there to be more names than just Eleni's etched on his bedpost. Seventeen and just the one sexual partner. What the shit was that all about, particularly as he has been watching porn since twelve, knows how to satisfy two women at a time, knows how girls arch their backs and grunt with pleasure. But all that stuff isn't real. Watching isn't doing. Doing is different. With Eleni he doesn't need dildos or leather. With her he isn't a spaz. Now his knife stays home.

On the second day the analysis of CCTV footage begins. There, at a bus stop, is the boy-man. And ten minutes later he is spotted passing *Game*, pausing for a moment to check the display. And then queuing outside the *Odeon*. There can be no doubt about this last sighting. His face is clearly shown in the high-definition recordings which also reveal the TV channel watched by the retired couple living in the warehouse conversion across the canal, the time they eat, the way they make love to lesbian blue movies.

Do not approach this youth

On the fifteenth day Alfie's mother is woken by a call. She grabs the phone. By the time DI Potter voices the words analysis, hard drive, brutality, she gets the drift.

He's not a bad boy, she explains, thoughts and sleeping-pill induced dreams interweaving. It's his leg, that's all. Disabled, bullied youth turns briefly to regrettable violence, then redeems himself. That's where this story heads, surely, to happy-ever-after.

Have you heard anything, any news, any sightings? Have you heard? Anything?

On day minus five Alf is at Eleni's, a home infused with the scent of moussaka and bouzouki strumming, where the stickiness of baklava lingers on the breath. Everything's going to be all right from now on. Everything's cool.

WHAT TIME ARE YOU
COMING HOME?
MUM X
17:18

why are you yelling?!!!!
17:35

yELLING? i DID NOT i JUST
ASKED A QUESTION? X
17:36

Oops. Any idea? X
17:37

Any idea Alfie? X
17:40

Any idea Alfie? xxxx
18:07

later..........
22:59

On the sixth day Alfie's mother checks her mobile phone, her answer phone, the post, her email, her *Facebook*, Alfie's *Facebook*. She wanders round the house, checks the garden, looks for little notes poked between paving slabs, snapped under windscreen wipers, jammed into the bark of the plum tree. A thread from his trousers, a footprint in a bed. A camera whirrs – chisst, chisst, chisst – as it follows her progress and she is tempted to flip it the bird. Instead she straightens her shoulders and heads back inside to check her mobile phone, the answer phone, her email, her *Facebook*, Alfie's *Facebook*.

Day minus four.
    On r bench xxxxx
    17:56

    Where u? xxxxx
    18:08

    Where r u?
    18:17

    ??????
    18.43

On the seventh day there is a confirmed sighting at Piccadilly Circus where Alf is spotted by his former science teacher. Ever wary of Alfred Parsons, Mr Gunter stepped into the gutter to let the lad pass. He seemed meek, Mr Gunter reported the following day, not at all the same lad he held in detention for spitting.

When questioned about the delay in coming forward, Mr Gunter wipes sweat from his forehead before admitting that perhaps the encounter had been a few hundred metres north of Piccadilly Circus, perhaps in Soho, outside Schwang, but please don't tell his wife. His sporadic visits to the sex club are all that have kept his marriage together these past fifteen years.

Subsequent enquiries in the area fail to locate Alf. The trail has gone cold.

On day minus two Alf confronts Eleni. The complete blank in communications. Why? Eleni blinks a lot. She half turns her face away. Why?

On day eight, the minute Alfie's mother hears he has been sighted for sure, she heads up to London. She checks his picture on her phone, the photo that pops up each time she dials his number. Even though his phone goes straight to the voicemail's full message, she keeps dialling five, six, seven times an hour. She looks at that picture all the train journey, worried that after the eternity of not seeing him she won't be able to recognise her son.

She stands beneath Eros, on exactly the spot Alfie might have stood twenty-four hours earlier and, even though it is stupid, she is tempted to bend down and check the pavement for a piece of his hair, or a nail he might have bitten off. She hates the delay caused by Mr Gunter's weakness for lap dancers, just as much as she hates the young men who walk past wearing skinny jeans, chatting as though there is nothing at all wrong.

The flick of a coat and the hint of a stooped head and she's off following. It could be him. She wants to yell out in great big capital letters for real now to attract his attention, shout till her sixteen-point font voice is heard throughout the city.

ALFIE! ALFIE! ALFIE!

She tails him up Shaftesbury Avenue, down Charing Cross Road, until somewhere near Temple he turns.

My son, she tells him. You look like my son.

The man shakes his head and he is nothing like Alfie, nothing at all.

On Blackfriars Bridge she stares into the tide sweeping upstream and understands that the only reason for her existing any longer is for Alfie to return to once this stupid misunderstanding has been sorted. He has to come home.

On day eight Alf makes his way down the steps outside Sea Containers House onto the Thames shore, where amber lights glisten on a discarded rubber sole, a comb, a shard of glass. He scuffs at a piece of blue pottery, stamps on a clay pipe bowl the river has failed to destroy. His coat, laden with rain, tugs him down and the lazy wind blows straight through him.

Under Blackfriars Bridge, dribbles of brackish water creep towards him and a shooting star slices through the night sky. He lights a match for warmth and lets it burn his fingers.

The day itself is warm. Alf has said he will be waiting on their bench. One last chat, Eleni agrees she owes him that much. He sits, elbows on knees, fingers clicking. He is ready, knows what to say. She arrives alone.

He's got a reputation, she says. Bit of a psycho.

Hey, he says, laughing it off. This is me you're talking about.

Yeah, she says, but you know.

They mock my leg, he tells her. What am I to do? Let them?

Yeah, she says. The leg.

Is that it? he says. It's over because of my leg?

More the psycho stuff, she says.

Fuck them, eh. He slaps his knuckles into the bench seat. And fuck you too if you believe them, Eleni.

And they go to the place, the one where they could have had sex without anyone seeing them, probably. And he has his blade with him again.

And Eleni? Eleni? If he can't have her then no one can. Fuck them. Fuck her. Fuck the whole fucking world.

Once upon a time there was a boy.

The Chair

Matthew alters the position of the second chair, three centimetres to the left, so that when Stephen reaches for his glass, he will have to turn his head a few degrees away from the sun setting behind Wawel Hill. That will be the correct angle.

Congealed air drifts in through the open window and, from the street below, a soft thud indicates Mrs Nowak is out, beating the dust from the rag mat that serves as the boot wipe at the communal entrance. A pause. Matthew waits for the rustle of her hand settling on her house-coated hip, her sigh that expects a response from him sitting at the window above.

"Good evening, Mrs Nowak," Matthew calls down.

The click of a stale mouth opening, as though after five months she is surprised that Matthew is still up here, watching the street, listening out.

"Good evening, Matthew."

A *foomfph* as the mat slaps back on the stone floor and the fizz of the brush against the paving slab doorstep.

"Your nephew arrives today." There is no question in Mrs Nowak's enquiry.

"Today," Matthew replies.

A fly lands on the rim of Stephen's glass. Matthew flicks it away, striking the glass with his nail so that in the moment of intense pain in his fingertip the glass rotates, teeters and claps back onto the table.

"Again and again," Mrs Nowak says, her voice louder as she turns to face his window.

"At last," Matthew corrects.

She can go back inside now, along the corridor to her apartment to tend to her pots or smalls or whatever it is that shortens her breath. He picks up the glass between his thumb and middle finger and repositions it to allow for the earth's rotation in the last three minutes. He checks Wawel Castle, the fall of its shadow down the hill's side. And from somewhere close by, from among these concrete-rendered terraces, he imagines he hears a young man laughing.

February. There should be snow outside muffling the trams' hisses and the clopping of the tourists' horse-drawn carriages. There should be a blast from the east, producing goose pimples and chapped nostrils. Instead, this universal weather belonging to any month and any place persists.

By the sink, the bottle of *Egri Bikaver* waits unopened. Matthew had considered his options on which wine to have ready. *Tokaji?* Too feminine, possibly. The finest sparkling *Pezsgo?* Too loaded with expectations of celebration. Instead he had bought *Egri Bikaver*, Bull's Blood. Traditional. Solid. No hint of anything other than two men who haven't seen each other for a while sharing a glass or two. No presumptions.

It is five thirty p.m., way past wine o'clock somewhere on the earth. Matthew clatters in the utensil drawer, shakes the handle in order that the corkscrew might rise to the top. He will let the wine breathe so that when Stephen arrives, it will be ready to gloop into the glasses.

"*Na zdrowie*," Matthew will say.

"It's been too long," Stephen will reply as he raises his glass.

Perhaps now that five months have passed, Matthew might check his phone for a text or email, something that might indicate the time of Stephen's promised arrival. He might even dial Stephen's number. Speak to him. Find out.

Again that laugh, or was it the potato peeler settling against the grater, or the squeak of his shoe on the tiled floor? He listens till he hears nothing but the buzzing in his ears.

A knock at the door, a triple rap, and Matthew drops the corkscrew on the floor. He is here. Already. Matthew should have stayed by the window with an ear to the squeal of a taxi's brakes, the slam of the door and the discussion in English about the ten zloty fare from the station. And yet he cannot go to the door, nor pick up the corkscrew, nor check the chair is just right. None of these he can do now that Stephen is on his doorstep.

Over the river Vistula, in Podgorze, on a blank wall created by a house demolition, a graffiti image of the cathedral bell masquerades as a megaphone preaching to entranced faces. Eyes closed, obedient. Lead us not into temptation. Deliver us from evil. Now that there has been a knock on his door, Matthew can only think of this painting and its portrayal of compliance. And he thinks of the dangers which have always faced anyone who finds themself in conflict with those who assign themselves authority: the Jews huddling together in the Nazi-established ghetto in Podgorze's streets; the Solidarity workers herding in the Gdansk shipyards, defying their communist repressors. He wants Stephen here to herd with against the amassed media he is crouching from.

Is it ten seconds since the knock on the door? Ten minutes?

"Yes?" he says.

"I have news, Matthew." Not Stephen, but Mrs Nowak.

There is no news concerning him that Mrs Nowak can know, nothing that can have seeped across Europe to Krakow.

"Not now," he says.

"If Stephen is arriving today eventually, you will want to hear."

She pronounces Stephen's name with a puff of air around the ph. Why had he ever provided her with a name to molest with her Polish tongue? The need to hear it spoken out loud, perhaps. The need for reassurance that, in the absence of any contact, Stephen still exists? And to say the lad is his nephew? Why not? He bends, picks up the corkscrew, places it by the Bull's Blood.

"Really?" he says and he finds the last syllable rises too high so that forces itself into the back of his mouth.

A pause.

"Matthew?"

He coughs out the blockage of air, walks to the door. And Mrs Nowak is there, standing at an angle, ready to leave, with her house-coat pocket, faded by years of dusters, billowing open.

"The train is not running. I heard it on the radio only now when I sat. So the buses come from the airport instead and that is extra time."

"Thank you," Matthew says.

She nods and, as she lays her hand on the wooden banister to turn down the stairs, he adds, "That is kind of you."

"It is OK."

Perhaps Matthew will pull on his hat and go for a walk, flaps down over his ears and cheeks, peak pulled out. Perhaps he will cross the lovers' bridge, check for new love locks, see where the wire has been cut away to remove those whose symbolism has outlived the reality. And then stride over to Podgorze and that graffiti, tell those white, bovine faces to listen up, hear the alternatives. He will take with him Stephen's texts, hold them up to the submissive mass to read, shove the gentle messages right in their faces.

"Life is never one story," he will yell. "See!"

But his phone remains in his suitcase, uncharged, because knowing that Stephen is no longer thinking of his lover teacher, his teacher of love, would be worse than imagining it.

The sun has set. The air is cold. Even with a delay caused by public transport failures there is no purpose now to Matthew's positioning of Stephen's chair. He picks up the glasses and places them back in the cupboard. And he sits in his first-floor apartment on Jozefa Street, his chair turned towards the open window and Wawel Castle.

Tomorrow will be the day he uncorks the wine.

Some Place to Eat

We were down by the Wey Navigation, where it passes the ruined priory at Newark. The flood plain. You know it? Just after that sweep down the hill by St Nicolas' Church? That's where we were. On the towpath. Standing.

Dad had this thing at that time. His head was always on to the next thing, and the next, so even though we were by the canal, he was talking about some pub he'd read up about. He wasn't committed to eating there, not until he saw what the place was like. The atmosphere.

This narrow boat chugged past, the Sally-May, with a dog running along its roof, barking a swan out of the way. All big and bold from five feet above. Dad looked at that boat and said, "Birmingham?"

He read that off the side. Birmingham? Like he'd never heard of the place.

"It's in the Midlands," I said.

"I know where Birmingham is."

I was fifteen. He forty-six. Not old, but some time ago he'd stopped picking up sticks to fight me with, and tumbling me over and over on the grass till I couldn't breathe. He'd stopped bothering me about brushing my teeth and drinking Coke. I'm not sure when all that had dropped off. Perhaps when he'd had to become a bit of Mum too.

Anyhow, we were right by the canal and he was saying he knew where Birmingham was without any smile. Next thing we'd be back to discussing this place to eat, like it was the only important thing he knew to talk about.

"Sorry," I said.

"Why are you sorry? Always sorry nowadays, you."

The Sally-May *futt-futted* off round the bend. I stepped forward to look after her and waited for Dad to call, *Careful you don't fall in*, like it was funny, like it had always been funny to say, *Careful you don't fall in* and then judder me and hold on to me like he'd saved my life. I was ready. If he touched me.

"Really?" he said.

Really my arse. Really what? Really it's OK to spend an afternoon talking about some place to eat.

So I did it. I stepped clear into the water. I'd like to say it was an elegant jump but in truth it was a slither and a bit of a yelp and ten tons of reeds wrapped around me till I was sitting on them, bum wet, top totally dry, facing a moorhen. And for what? Complete twat.

Except there was no *What have I said?* or *I told you so*. There wasn't anything. So I sat, being absorbed into the canal because the wanker did not say a sodding thing. Could talk for years about some stupid menu he might never eat, but not say anything at all.

In the end ... like there's ever an end to anything. Except when someone dies. Is that really an end though? Anyhow, a short while later, I decided to sort myself out and that's when the fun started. Loads of weaving and waving and slipping till I was well over my waist.

"Help, Dad!" He didn't move. "Why won't you help?"

And I swear to God he glanced at me for an instant. I swear he did. But if he did glance, that was all.

I don't know how I got out because one minute I was up to my waist in the Sally-May's wake with the Wey's wildlife paddling round me, and the next I was dripping next to him, while he stared off at the sky, following something that had flown.

"No," he said. Just like that. "No."

"No what, Dad?" I said.

I didn't want to touch him. I was wet, see. Wet and a bit cold.

"No what?"

He looked down at my trousers. He should have shouted, or he should have laughed. He should have done what Mum would have done. I'd been in the water. I'd arsed around. Messed. Got wet.

"Dad?"

"What are you talking about?" he said.

I'm sorry, I wanted say. Sorry. But my mouth was clenched with cold.

Letters from Prague

Hotel Koruna

Opatovicka

Prague

24th July 2014

Dear Tomas,

I am in Prague! Surprised? I am. I'm here for the weekend, till Sunday, arriving this morning. Yesterday, I had no idea I would be here. And now I don't know what to think, or do. We flew in to Ruzyne Airport early this morning, came into the city by bus. Rob commented on the communist prefab flats lining the route, on the poor things living in them.

We drank coffee in the Old Town Square, listening to the horses clattering their shoes against the cobbles while they waited for their carriages to be hired. Around me swirled French and German, Russian, Japanese and Czech. I heard them all and reminded myself that I shouldn't understand any of them. And we watched the tourists crowding round the astrological clock to hear it chime on the hour. I was delighted by the automata, as required. This is my birthday treat, Tomas. I'm 50!

Our hotel's fine. An adequate room, twin beds, and I am told the water will be hot later - some things don't change. Rob skipped thorough the TV channels, just the basic, a few barely lingered upon Czech channels, but we have *Eurosport* in German, that's new. He turned it off and went out to 'orientate' himself in the Kafka Bar opposite, pleased to have come up with such a treat for my birthday, delighted to have kept it a secret from me.

I have a headache - the plane journey, the surprise - so I've stayed here to rest. It's been a long time, Tomas.

Yours, Carolyn.

Outside Prague Castle

25th July 2014

Dear Tomas,

A water tank has just passed, spraying the heated pavements. The dull odour of wet dust fills the air. The guard stands his place despite a Japanese girl's attempt to get him to speak or move while her photograph is taken painfully slowly. We are waiting for the changing of the guard. Rob is excited. This first venture into the former Eastern Bloc - that scary place from his childhood - fascinates him.

I am to wait here, sitting on the wall, while he tries to find a bottle of water. We're both thirsty, but I mustn't miss the changing of the guard. Rob's like that - he wants to see it, so I mustn't miss it. Kind, thoughtful, yet always based on the premise that I will want what he wants, like this weekend.

But you won't know about Rob. We married in 1990, have two children, Ben, 24, and Ella, 20. Ben's a teacher and Ella's at university, studying European Modern Languages. I tell everyone I don't know where she gets her aptitude from. Some lies I wish I had never begun because I would like to be able to discuss Brecht with her in German, and Maupassant in French, and Havel's plays in Czech, just like you and I did once.

And music! I'd forgotten that this is a city of music. It is everywhere, every street corner, every church. There is a group of French lads here with dreadlocks, Ben's sort of age. They were in the Old Town Square this morning as we passed through, each with an instrument - violin, saxophone, drum, trumpet - and they laughed as they played Vivaldi's *Summer*. Such fun.

Ah, I hear the soldiers' boot heels skittering across the cobbles. The guards are about to change. And Rob is back with water.

Yours, Carolyn.

Hotel Koruna

Opatovicka

Prague

25th July 2014

Dear Tomas,

It is 2 am. Outside the city is amber bright. Next to me Rob sleeps gently, his arm flopped off the bed, his breathing noisy, on the edge of a snore. I woke with a start ten minutes ago, realising that my last letter might have caused you to jump to a conclusion. You were good at picking apart details. Perfect for your job.

Ben is Rob's child. Despite that night in Vienna in '89, that last meeting, I am certain. Does that make you happy? Sad? Do you care?

There, it's said now.

We went to see *Alice's Adventures* at the Black Light Theatre this evening — see how readily I write that name in English, as easily I write these letters — and we watched the spectacle of flying and optical jokes in ultraviolet light. At one point Alice knelt, holding a candle and the flame moved off, and another, and another, a coronet of flames circling her head, until each tiny light rejoined the main candle. I wondered about that being a metaphor for you, me and the others back then, each moving off independently, each part of a whole. I believe you would have enjoyed the metaphor discussion, dear Tomas, had we been able to have it.

Afterwards, Rob and I stood on Charles Bridge. The stalls had packed away their gaudy pictures of Prague and photos of the city in the snow and Bohemian glass jewellery. The lights from the castle glinted on the Vltava. And I thought how this is my city and, as Rob linked his arm through mine and kissed me on the cheek, I did not know where I belonged.

Tomorrow (today!) we visit Josefov. We have to do the synagogues, Rob says, like we did the Charles Bridge and the arty shops of Kampa. And he is right. The fascist-inflicted pain is what I must remember now.

It is night. I must sleep.

Yours, Carolyn.

Rose Garden

Petrin Hill

26th July 2014

Tomas,

Oh God, the horror! Those innocent pictures drawn by the children killed in the camps - mother and father, sisters and brothers, all with saucer smiles, lined up in front of a house with yellow sun rays spearing the air above them. The sort of picture every child draws. Pictures Ben and Ella drew. And yet, as these children chewed their tongues in concentration and pushed their hair back behind their ear, they had no idea their names would end up carved into stone pillars in the room next door among the columns and columns of the gassed, or that their parents would not stand next to them forever, hand in hand, smiling.

The fight was right, Tomas. That can never be allowed to happen again.

And yet... and yet...

We then visited the memorial to those who died under communism. A row of statues of men stretching back, the one at the front whole, then each subsequent statue missing a tiny bit of his body until the one at the back is not recognisable as a man at all, a representation of the complete dehumanisation of an individual.

What is the difference?

In Wenceslas Square, after the synagogues and the memorial, we attached ourselves to an American tour group and listened to the story of the '89 Velvet Revolution, of Václav Havel's balcony speech. Rob marvelled and repeated sections, not knowing that he is recounting my own history.

You came looking for me after '89, I know. But everything was uncertain. Lines of communication suddenly closed. So what then of our role to 'contribute towards the downfall of capitalism' when my country had embraced that enemy? Where did I fit?

I was trained to be invisible. I could walk on sand and leave no footprints, pass along a street and be un-remarked upon. A social chameleon is what you'd made of me. And, Tomas, I was pregnant with another man's child - that's how deep my entrenchment in British society had become.

I was good by then, better than you could ever have known. I acquired a new passport, destroyed my papers and my one-time decoding pads. I disappeared for the second time in my life. I hid so that my child and I could have stability, certainty.

Here I am, lying in the shade of a tree in the Rose Garden on Petrin Hill, watching a triangle of sun creep across my foot. Rob has gone to fetch ice creams - he says he didn't imagine it being this hot here. The scent of roses infuses the air around me and a man, who loves me enough to bring me to Prague as a birthday surprise, fetches me an ice cream, while all I can hear is my mother crying goodbye in our communist prefab flat. 'Just for a little while,' I told her, when in truth I had promised a lifetime commitment to the StB.

He woke last night just as I finished writing to you. I'm keeping a diary, that's what I told him. He thinks the idea's charming. He thinks I want to log each minute as his gift is perfect. He's a good man, but you can tell that from what I write.

Will you receive these letters, Tomas? Will I send them?

Your Karolina.

Prague Airport

27th August 2014

Dearest Tomas,

I have faith that I will leave the Czech Republic just as easily as I entered four days ago - no system to track down long-lost agents picked me up then. See, I am nothing to this country. But to you, Tomas? Do you remember me, Karolina, the student with a gift for languages, the woman you trained for three years, the lover you broke the rules with?

Well, I am no longer her. And now, after this weekend, I am no longer Carolyn Pryce either.

Last night, in our twin-bedded hotel room, I spoke to Rob about our future together. He was surprised, staggered, appalled. He never had any idea that I might not love him as much as he loves me. Maybe I can't love anyone or anything, I told him. He doesn't know where all this has come from and I cannot begin to tell him. There has been so much deceit that even beginning to explain will convince him he must abandon this woman he never knew at all.

I am not a die-hard communist, Tomas. I was a patriot of my time. Ideals die. Secrets imprison intimacy, smother life. And you are the only person I can say all this to, a fellow ghost in a half-world.

Rob won't look at me. I have hurt him.

Prague draws me to her. Is it time to come home, Tomas? Or is it time to go home? What would you, my teacher, my lover, advise?

All I know is that I will forever be your Karolina.

Heading West

The wind sings to itself as Leo marches along the side of the A303. He is tempted to join in, make up words in time to the beat of the wind and the rhythm of his steps. I love to, I, oh woe, oh tum. Perhaps not. Still, whether he joins it or not, the wind is singing.

A *parp* on a driver's horn. Leo raises his cap. Indeed, Sir, a very fine evening. But the Seat has passed on down the road towards Honiton. Leo feels in his pocket. There, the biscuit that fell off his saucer as the lass slopped his tea down at the diner.

"I did my best," she said.

"And your best is surely good enough."

The tea hadn't been all that though. Not quite the *Kenya Milima Orthodox* he left on the kitchen table for Matilda. Leo looks back in the direction of Andover and is momentarily blinded by headlights and dizzied by the buffet of the wind from a passing van. His eyes smart.

Matilda.

He rips the plastic wrapper open and pops the biscuit whole into his mouth.

A hubcap. A small bag with its handles tied. A glove of the gardening type. Leo staggers on a tussock and straightens. A clear plastic bottle of something. He backs up, takes a run and hoofs it into the open goal. Stadium lights, the roar roar roar of delight. A Mexican wave. If his legs were up to it, he would fall to his knees, raise his arms and thank God. Instead, with the A303 behind him, he lets the evening's moisture settle on his face.

A car pulls up twenty yards or so ahead of him. Perhaps someone has been alarmed by the stoopy fellow standing in the dark with his arms in the air on the side of an A-road. Ah well. He steps onto the even tarmac, less perilous than the verge for one of a certain age, and with a hip, and the other.

"You all right?" a young man, who might in fact be a young woman, leans across to ask.

The heat drifting out through the window strokes Leo's face and he is reminded of a certain hand's softness.

"Amazing evening," he replies. "Truly wonderful."

"It's three in the morning."

"There isn't much I can do about that." Leo smiles. God handles the time thing, He orders events and spaces them out according to some what? Some whim perhaps? Because if there's a plan He's working to, it surely needs adjustment.

The lad/lass shoves the creaking car door open.

"I'll drop you at the next services," it says. "Somewhere warm."

Leo pauses. The thing about taking a walk to the seaside is that it's as much about the walk as arriving at the beach. But seeing as this youngster has bothered to stop for a doddery old git, Leo finds that the wind's tune has become nothing other than an intermittent blast, and his eyes appear to be persisting with their foolish watering. The journey's the thing, he decides, not the walking. No, the walking's irrelevant.

"Truly kind." He removes a box from the passenger seat to sit and rests one foot on top of the other to avoid a brown paper bag and a drink can in the foot well. With the box on his lap, Leo finds that, all things considered, the car is rather comfortable.

"I was just thinking about you," the young folk says.

Now that the streetlights are glancing across the person's face, Leo sees that she is definitely a girl, probably.

"About me?"

"Not about you, as such." It checks the rear-view mirror. "More about, God, I don't know. More about everyone, I guess. More about how we all hang together. More about how if, like, there was no one to clean my water, then I'd die, so I need that person even though I don't know them."

There is a lump in the seat. Leo wriggles away from it.

"That's a lot to be dwelling on," he says.

The young person shrugs. "My radio's broken," it says.

The box has sharp cardboard corners. Neatly delineated uprights. There is something pleasing about the precise engineering of the box among the debris in the car, something that speaks of an ordered world, of purpose in chaos.

"I'm heading to the seaside," Leo says.

"Bit late for that."

Yes, definitely a girl. But what about that jawline?

"Possibly." Leo leans forward slightly to catch an alternative angle. "It was just an idea."

The car's smell is mid-way between sweet and must, something manufactured and something lived in, like the result of powder rubbed in Matilda's armpits. Fresh as a daisy, my treasure. Fit to meet the queen.

"Nasty cough," the lass/lad says.

"I borrowed it some time back." Leo turns to the window in case the youngster catches sight of his smile. He and Matilda don't give each other coughs and colds, they borrow them from each other. That way, when one has had too much of some ailment — a headache, a tummy ache, the shivers - the other can take it for a while to allow the sunshine to blast over their lover's easy skin and soul, to alleviate the drowning.

Outside is orange-black. Strange how, even though he is in the warm and insulated from the joyful wind, his eyes can't seem to stop this wretched seeping. He lays the back of his hand on his cheeks to mop up the dampness.

"This is a very fine vehicle." Leo tries to stretch his leg a little to ease the gammy hip he never let on to Matilda about - one can only borrow so much - but the can crunches beneath his feet and there's something soft. A coat maybe. No need to get grubby shoes on that.

The youngster murmurs, or perhaps it simply clears its throat.

"I hope I'm not taking you out of your way," Leo says. "But it is jolly pleasant to sit."

The click click click of the indicator and the car swings out from behind a van.

"I feel quite the prince in his carriage." Undoubtedly the swaying in a grand coach would be just as in this car.

"It's a Fiesta. Ninety-six," the youngster says with a confidence in both year and model that convinces Leo that he must be being driven by a boy.

They swing back in and something inside the box swooshes and thuds into the side. Perhaps Leo should have placed it on the back seat, but the driver hasn't said anything and to turn to peer behind seems somewhat intrusive. The road ahead is cave-black. No streetlights here, just a tunnel of darkness.

"Quite a party." Leo says, and as he laughs at his linguistic joke the pain he borrowed from Matilda grips his stomach, deep and burrowing and sharp. For a moment he cannot think about breathing, and even the image of the sunrise and the beach that he holds in reserve for these moments, blurs into grey invisibility.

"You can help yourself to some of that cake if you're hungry," the youngster checks the wing mirror.

The pain inside Leo pauses, then returns as an ache. Something uncomfortably dull. Something that will not behave.

"In the box," the lass/lad says. "It's nice."

"It's very kind of you to pick me up like some sort of hitcher, young -" Leo waits.

"Alex."

"Indeed," Leo says, for why wouldn't this person have a name that could so equally be shared by a man wielding a spanner and a woman dressed in chiffon that wafts around her and bears her up on the breeze, floating her until she glides through the cotton wool clouds into the beautiful sunshine, away into the sky bluer than any blue that anyone living has ever seen. For a moment Leo looks up and sees his Matilda kicking her legs as she floats off, not wanting the air to take her, shouting out in resentment, "Not yet!"

That ache is still there, except it's everywhere, in his arms and in his throat, even in his willy.

"It's not poisoned," Alex says.

Leo holds his breath, five, eight, ten seconds. A car approaches from the opposite direction and for a moment the Fiesta is full of the flare of its lights and thuds of the steady beat of some drum that vibrates through the car and his body, until Leo is certain it will reset the rhythm of his heart.

"What the actual fuck?" The youngster peers in both wing mirrors then the rear-view mirror.

"Do you think God teases us?" Leo asks.

"Fuck!" Alex says.

Ah well. Leo opens the box and in the harsh white light reflected from the wing mirror he sees the letters '*n Voyage*' piped in blue on the remaining quarter of a fruit cake. Now his pesky stomach isn't diverting him, Leo does feel a bit peckish.

"Sorry. Blinded me, the bastard," Alex says.

"I was eighty-two last week," Leo says. "You wouldn't think it, would you? Eighty-two and running away to the seaside."

"Do you want a drink or something? For that cough?"

"No, siree. I'll keep hold of this cough, if you don't mind." It doesn't need passing on any further. "Shall I just break a piece off?"

Alex is wearing jeans with a hole in the knee, through which pokes the whitest of white skin, almost the shimmer of mother of pearl. And his/her t-shirt droops at the sleeve where a thread hangs down. Leo holds out a collection of icing and marzipan and crumbs surrounding currents, and she/he bends his/her head to eat out of Leo's palm. The lips nuzzle and break away and Leo is left trying to remember the sensation, just as he tries to remember Matilda's hug, where her arms rested. Behind his back? Up over his shoulders? Clutching her hands against his body, or holding on to each other?

Leo wipes his hand on his trousers. He might have done anything with that hand: not washed it since peeing, or brushing away the remnants of beans on toast, or holding that cloth over Matilda's face. How is this person to trust that hand when she/he doesn't know what it has done? He digs his fingers into the cake and pulls off a hunk and eats as the youngster has just eaten, like a horse from a nosebag.

A lorry the size of a factory rumbles past. Ahead, the join between the Somerset hills and the sky is lightening, silhouetting a clump of trees. A sign. Half a mile to some village beginning with B and to Local Services.

"What's with the seaside?" Alex doesn't indicate to pull off, just keeps rolling along the A303.

"The fancy took me." Leo picks at a bit more cake.

"Alone?" Alex turns and Leo becomes convinced that she is a girl. A girl who, as the natural light surrounds her, has become slight, ethereal.

"As alone as I am," Leo says and he thinks of the candle he left burning, the water by Matilda's bed, and he thinks how long, long ago that all was, before the wind that swept two seasons of sun and rain through in a day, before the air cleared, before dusk.

"Where are you travelling?" Leo asks.

"Home."

"Been away long?"

"Sort of."

And as Leo settles back in his seat, he feels the lump again and remembers now that's how Matilda's hand rested on his back, just a little pressure from the ball of her palm, and how the other hand held his head and how, as he leant over her, he stole the cramping pain she refused to let him borrow so that she could snuggle back into his rolled-up dressing gown. And as he pulled away, he squeezed one of her hands round the cloth to make-believe his hand was still there, and placed the other under the blankets. And he put the tea on the kitchen table, just in case. And because God spreads out time differently for everyone, because today could be yesterday, could be next year, he decided what fun it would be to head to the sea where he would find Matilda paddling in that blue-flowered costume, with the skirt round her hips.

The tarmac beneath the wheels swells an invisible song and the *tick tick* of indicator beats. Ho hum. Tum-ti-tuuum, and the living is easy.

"It'll be good to get home," he believes he says to Alex, but perhaps he sings.

And perhaps the youngster replies in kind, or perhaps it is the wind hissing through some gap somewhere that resonates like an Aeolian harp, but as all the words Leo has ever sung meld into an awesome melody, Matilda sings with him in harmony.

A Contemplation of Rain and Ducks

The rain kept on raining. Geraldine kicked at the puddles. "Fuck this weather," she said. "Fit for fucking ducks." A drake mallard waddled onto the pathway.

"Good morning, Geraldine," he said.

"Fucking great," Geraldine said. "A talking duck."

"*Deux langues*," he elaborated.

"No idea what you're saying."

She flicked the rain drops off her plastic raincoat and sat on the seat overlooking the pond, grinding her heels into the sodden mud beneath her feet.

"*Vous ne parlez pas le francais?*" The duck settled itself down on the path in front of her with a ripple of wing feathers.

Geraldine pulled her *Thermos* from her coat pocket and poured the room temperature merlot into the metal cup.

"Me thinks you are in need of company," the duck said.

"Me thinks you can fuck off, duck."

"Call me Harold," Harold advised. "Duck is so general."

The smooth wine hit the back of her throat with a satisfying kick.

"Fuck," she said.

"As you like," Harold said. "*Commes vous voulez*."

"Speak anything other than French?" Geraldine asked.

"But of course," Harold said. "I speak English."

"OK, French and English?"

"I'd have thought that was quite enough for a duck."

The rain started again, great dollops of it thumping down on the ground, sending out coronas of mud. It gathered in the turn up of her hood and dribbled down the side of her cheek.

"And now you are crying," Harold said.

Somehow, a talking duck who mistook cold rainwater for sadness vexed Geraldine.

"I'll give you a good kick if you don't shut up," she said.

"But why? I am a simple duck."

Geraldine tsked and shook her head. Other ducks drifted round the pond, feathers slightly ruffled, necks concertinaed into their bodies while shrapnel rain blasted around them. Even the ducks, for whom this weather was fit, weren't enjoying the day. Geraldine took another sip, wondering whether the wine would mellow her or whether it would grip at her stomach and prance round her head.

"Do you have nothing to say to me when I'm making such an effort to be companionable?" Harold asked.

She shook her head. The duck looked affronted.

"A plain little duck? *Harold le petit canard?*" He turned his head away. Shit, even a duck could make her feel guilty.

"I'm not going to call you Harold," she said. "That's just madness."

Geraldine sipped her way through a cup of wine, and as she did so she considered the rain and the clouds and the prevailing wind conditions. And as her second cup emptied, she found herself musing on the accuracy of weather forecasting using seaweed and fir cones, which morphed, for some reason, into a contemplation of the last successful invasion mainland Britain.

"Are you taking the piss, by any chance?" she asked the duck, who had sat silently throughout.

"*Comment?*" he replied.

"Coming over here and speaking French. Is that in anyway trying to rub my nose in the history of this island?"

"*Oooo la la,*" Harold said. "I am merely a duck, not a conqueror."

"One who speaks French."

"And English," he reminded her. "For us that is normal. We travel far." Geraldine shrugged. That did make sense. "So," Harold asked. "Now we're speaking, why the sadness?"

"What sadness?"

"The sadness that lurks beneath the rain hood, and the sadness that hides in your shoes. The sadness that trails you like a dark cloud, floating six inches behind your shoulder."

Geraldine glanced behind her. "How could I possibly tell a duck?" she said.

"No one else here to tell." Again, there was irritating logic in the duck's words.

"I am sad because my mum died. And I am sad because my carpet is threadbare and my job is shit but it's coming to an end, which makes me want it. And I am sad because I broke a jam jar this morning. And I am sad because these shoes that I loved mean nothing to me, not a thing. And I am sad because I am in the park in the rain, drinking wine that makes nothing go away, talking to a bilingual duck who wants to be called Harold."

The duck nodded. "Would it cheer you up if you could call me whatever you like?" he asked. "The Harold thing is just an affectation. I'm not that married to it."

Lifetime

From: gill.hardcastle@adh.freedom.com

To: whostheman@fasttmail.co.uk

Sent: Thursday, June 12, 2007 11:32 PM

Subject: Apologies

Dear Who's The Man,

I have just arrived home riven with guilt at my earlier behaviour towards you. I should certainly not have said that *The Garden at Dawn* bore no resemblance to any work that Rothko had ever completed or even contemplated. Nor should I have expanded my ill-considered opinion by adding that any comparison with Rousseau's finely comic jungle paintings was laughable. I will not blame the sauvignon blanc, as I have passed the age for blaming poor behaviour on alcohol consumption which, just for the record, was moderate in any case. Rather, it was my perhaps my interest in you and your opinions that pushed me to challenge you until what might be considered to be the point of rudeness.

Suffice it to say, I apologise fully for my remarks which, even had you not been the artist, were inappropriate to make to a stranger... although to call you a stranger seems odd as I feel I know you better than someone I just happened to meet at an exhibition this evening.

All that is left for me to say is that I wish you every success in your future career.

Yours,

Gill Hardcastle.

From: whostheman@fasttmail.co.uk

To: gill.hardcastle@adh.freedom.com

Sent: Friday, June 20, 2007 10:01 AM

Subject: RE: Apologies

hi gill. flatmates girlfriend moved out, big hassle as she took his wireless router so couldn't reply sooner. hey, fair enough about not seeing any of rousseaus naivety in the garden at dawn, but it got you looking at my painting even if u didn't like it. and the rothko comparison was meant to be concerned with the meditative effects i intended the light to have, that's all, no delusions of grandeur!! i enjoyed our talk - if artists can't have full and frank discussions, who can?

whos the man!

ps are we strangers?

From: gill.hardcastle@adh.freedom.com
To: whostheman@fasttmail.co.uk
Sent: Saturday, June 21, 2007 9:08 AM
Subject: RE: Apologies

Dear Who's The Man,

I feel rather formal starting my emails like this. Unlike the rest of my generation, I have stood out against using email, preferring the old-fashioned standards required of letter writing and, perhaps, the romance associated with receiving handwritten post. I now see how out of date and irrelevant that has become, particularly as I only have your email address and, I am ashamed to admit, not even your name.

I was pleased to receive your email accepting my apology, although I certainly didn't expect one. My comments at the exhibition were out of character, but maybe our earlier chat, when we bumped into each other by the rather disconcerting paintings *Jail-bait* and *Hard Times*, had relaxed me in your company. Although I would never have presumed that you'd reply to my email, I did wonder whether I might have reconfirmed for you that anyone over 40 has a closed mind and heart when it comes to art created today. Rest assured on this point; having talked with you if my mind had been at all closed, it is now reopened. Thank you for that.

And now that I understand more fully the reference to Rothko, yes, I do believe the light may have held some of the calmness his paintings inspire. I should have allowed you to make that point fully when we were standing in front of your painting so I could consider it properly.

How's your work going now? I hope you've managed to get through that 'artist's block' you mentioned.

Yours, Gill

From: whostheman@fasttmail.co.uk
To: gill.hardcastle@adh.freedom.com
Sent: Saturday, June 21, 2007 11:01 AM
Subject: RE: Apologies

thanks for asking gill. artists block still seriously in place, seriously blockading every thought that comes to mind. every time a hint of an idea comes to me, my internal critic shoots it down. it's been done before, or i couldn't do it as well as so and so (such as the light in the garden at dawn which had none of the mesmerising effects rothko could create - you were sooo right there!), or so many other reasons why i shouldn't even bother putting brush to canvas. i think i may never paint again. seriously. and i painted the garden in 3 hours and which makes it totally weird that that was the one selected for the exhibition. why can't i just get on and paint for another 3 hours? whos the man.

From: gill.hardcastle@adh.freedom.com
To: whostheman@fasttmail.co.uk
Sent: Sunday, June 22, 2007 10:24 PM
Subject: RE: Apologies
Hello Who's the Man,

Oh dear. Now I feel as though my comments at the exhibition were not only rude but also destructive.

Just an observation however: you say you completed *The Garden at Dawn* in three hours. Can the previous years of experience and study be removed from that time scale? Did that picture not take you a lifetime to complete?

Kind regards, Gill

P.S. I have tried a rather less formal greeting; I realised how stuffy I was sounding and I'm really not stuffy at all, just unused to communicating informally with the written word.

From: whostheman@fasttmail.co.uk
To: gill.hardcastle@adh.freedom.com
Sent: Tuesday, June 24, 2007 12:07 PM
Subject: RE: Apologies

hey gill. yes and no. yes, telling me just how i'd failed to emulate an artist i've long been a fan of didn't help. and no, i was already as stuck as a duck in the muck before you told me what you thought of my attempt. but now you've got me thinking. has this email taken a lifetime to write? would a dot or perhaps even just the thought of a piece of work not take a lifetime to come up with. i feel like a face of my artists block has just had a groove taken out of it with a chisel. what's the sculpture inside though? fancy a drink sometime to discuss?

whos the man.

ps you, stuffy? you forget i've met you!

From: gill.hardcastle@adh.freedom.com
To: whostheman@fasttmail.co.uk
Sent: Thursday, June 26, 2007 7:12 PM
Subject: RE: Apologies

Hello Who's the Man,

Firstly, in many ways you're right, that email was written using all the experience you have had in life. But it contains such a small part of that experience that I'm sure it demonstrates only a very small part of your abilities and, as such, is not a notable work. I fear the same criticism would apply to a dot, however conscientiously painted! That having been said, I am delighted that something I said might have started you off on a path which may produce new ideas for your work.

Secondly, I'm not sure that it would be appropriate to meet for a drink.

And finally, as we have come this far together, who is the man? Do you have a name?

Kind regards, Gill

From: whostheman@fasttmail.co.uk
To: gill.hardcastle@adh.freedom.com
Sent: Friday, June 27, 2007 3:01 AM
Subject: RE: Apologies

Dear Gill,

See, I've gained further experience in life and hence altered the way I start my emails too! But now you've gone and muddied the waters. First you say that a dot, even though painted following my lifetime of experiences, wouldn't be noteworthy when it's my first idea in months. And then just when I want to discuss this very idea with you, you question the appropriateness of meeting for a drink, why?

whos the man.

PS you want to know who the man is? Meet me!

From: gill.hardcastle@adh.freedom.com
To: whostheman@fasttmail.co.uk
Sent: Friday, June 27, 2007 8:32 PM
Subject: RE: Apologies

Hello there,

I asked myself after I sent my last email why I thought it might be inappropriate for me to meet you for a drink and came to the conclusion that it was because I am probably 20 years older than you. And the problem with that is ... well, I'm unsure, but I have in the past associated a drink with romance which would be inappropriate. I have grown comfortable our email relationship and wouldn't want to spoil it. Perhaps we can consider the issues of how we bring life's experience to art through this medium and thus help you carve a masterpiece from your artist's block.

Yours, Gill.

From: whostheman@fasttmail.co.uk
To: gill.hardcastle@adh.freedom.com
Sent: Friday, June 27, 2007 8:59 PM
Subject: RE: Apologies

Hi Gill - I'm not trying to get into your knickers! Not that you're not an attractive woman and I know many men must have wanted to because you are desirable. And whatever you say about being older you certainly don't look old. And now I don't know what I'm trying to say and have probably messed up and you won't reply to this. I don't find writing easy so it's not the best way for me to consider life, the universe and everything. And in any case, I just fancied chatting over the idea you raised, not with any ulterior motive in mind. Who's the man?

From: gill.hardcastle@adh.freedom.com
To: whostheman@fasttmail.co.uk
Sent: Monday, June 30, 2007 1:43 PM
Subject: RE: Apologies

Hello Who's the Man.

Oh dear, I got that wrong too; I didn't mean that you must fancy me. I would never presume such a thing. OK then, here's the deal; you tell me your name and I'll meet up with you.

Yours, Gill.

From: whostheman@fasttmail.co.uk
To: gill.hardcastle@adh.freedom.com
Sent: Monday, June 30, 2007 3:01 PM
Subject: RE: Apologies

Frederick James Ponting. National Gallery Café. Thursday 2.30pm. C U there!

From: whostheman@fasttmail.co.uk
To: gill.hardcastle@adh.freedom.com
Sent: Thursday, July 3, 2007 11:57 PM
Subject: RE: Apologies

Thanks for a lovely afternoon and evening Gill. I usually find it hard to put into words my thoughts on things that interest and inspire me which is probably why I've taken to painting as a form of expression. But with you I seem to be able to say everything in the only way I know how and you understand it all which, hey, is why I gave you my email address in the first place! I hope I didn't ramble on and bore you this afternoon. And I hope the rest of our time together didn't bore you either — it certainly didn't bore me! What a wonderful discussion, what a wonderful time, what a wonderful, wonderful woman! When can I see you again? Fred xxx

From: whostheman@fasttmail.co.uk
To: gill.hardcastle@adh.freedom.com
Sent: Friday, July 4, 2007 10:01 AM
Subject: RE: Apologies

Gill! Are you out there? I have no other way of contacting you — no phone number, no address. I'm worried. Did you get home OK? Have I upset you? Sorry, sorry. Fred xxx

From: whostheman@fasttmail.co.uk
To: gill.hardcastle@adh.freedom.com
Sent: Friday, July 4, 2007 12:31 PM
Subject: RE: Apologies

Gill,

So I lied when I said I didn't want to get into your knickers. We can forget all that if you want, even though it was an experience I never want to forget. Please just email me that you're OK.

Love Fred xxx

From: gill.hardcastle@adh.freedom.com
To: whostheman@fasttmail.co.uk
Sent: Saturday, July 5, 2007 3:35 PM
Subject: RE: Apologies

Dear Fred,

I loved our chat at the National Café and we did have a wonderful time wandering around the National together. And thank you for taking me back to your flat to see *The Garden at Dawn* again so I could reconsider the Rothko comparison. And the rest of the evening was neither upsetting nor anything for you to apologise for. Indeed it was stunningly enjoyable. But ...

From: whostheman@fasttmail.co.uk
To: gill.hardcastle@adh.freedom.com
Sent: Saturday, July 5, 2007 5:36 PM
Subject: RE: Apologies

.. but what? Gill, I miss our email conversations. I miss you. xxx

From: gill.hardcastle@adh.freedom.com
To: whostheman@fasttmail.co.uk
Sent: Monday, July 7, 2007 4:26 PM
Subject: RE: Apologies

Dear Fred,

I am 22 years older than you. You need to find someone nearer your own age, someone who'll give you children and who'll grow old with you, not be a pensioner when you're in your prime. However much you think you care for me now, you will in time want something I cannot give you. This will pass. That much is certain. Thank you for wonderful memories.

Regards, Gill.

From: whostheman@fasttmail.co.uk

To: gill.hardcastle@adh.freedom.com

Sent: Monday, July 7, 2007 4.58 PM

Subject: RE: Apologies

I don't want children. I want someone I can talk to. I want you.
Fred xxx

From: whostheman@fasttmail.co.uk

To: gill.hardcastle@adh.freedom.com

Sent: Tuesday, July 8, 2007 5:01 AM

Subject: RE: Apologies

Please Gill!

From: whostheman@fasttmail.co.uk

To: gill.hardcastle@adh.freedom.com

Sent: Wednesday, July 9, 2007 10:04 AM

Subject: RE: Apologies

Gill, Do you not care for me at all? Do you want me to go away?
Fred xx

From: gill.hardcastle@adh.freedom.com

To: whostheman@fasttmail.co.uk

Sent: Friday, July 11, 2007 7:32 PM

Subject: RE: Apologies

Dearest Fred,

I apologise, again; I should never have allowed that kiss or what it led to. I'm sorry if you misinterpreted this action, which indeed is very misinterpretable. I never wanted to taint you with my cynicism born from too many heart breaks, another one of which would be the inevitable conclusion for us, I fear. Yet now I have given you cause to generate your own cynicism and I bitterly regret that.

Of course I care; how could I not. I'm doing this right now because I care.

I wish you a wonderful life. Paint and keep painting. Rothko and Rousseau weren't that great that they are out of your reach. Enjoy it!

Yours, Gill.

From: whostheman@fasttmail.co.uk
To: gill.hardcastle@adh.freedom.com
Sent: Friday, July 11, 2007 9:01 PM
Subject: RE: Apologies

Dearest dearest Gill,

I will go away, not because I want to but because you've asked me to and because a person who loves someone does what they ask.

What more can anyone do for the person they love?

Ever yours, Fred.

From: whostheman@fasttmail.co.uk
To: Many
Sent: Friday, January 16, 2009 10:01 AM
Subject: Lifetime

You are cordially invited to an exhibition of my work entitled *Lifetime* at the Hilborough Gallery, Monday 19th January — Friday 30th January.

"A remarkable range of paintings from a simple dot on a canvas to the complex and compelling *Unrequited*. The expression on the young man's face in this painting says everything that anyone who has ever loved and lost has felt." - Modern Artist.

Frederick J. Ponting

Voices

Francis hunkers down in a gap in the hedge and watches the sparkles glistening off his old primary school swimming pool. Behind him in the rec, Bean and Smith are shouting his name, like they really want him to come out and share their roll-up.

"Fraaaancis."

Francis imagines Bean drawing out the word on a stream of smoke.

"Oh Fraaaaaan." The word chokes in Bean's throat and Smith laughs.

They are both so fucking funny. Fuck them. A branch of dead holly leaves hangs off Francis's leg. Fuck that too. He pulls out the spikes and smears away the droplets of blood. Sweat runs down the side of his face and onto the end of his nose, like a tear. He bends forward to shake it off. Christ, it's hot. He grips hold of the chain-link fence embedded in the hedge and watches the breeze ripple the pool's surface.

Why had he run? Red rag to a bull. He should have walked away, just like nothing they said mattered. Water off a duck's back.

"Saaaain-t Francis," Smith had started out of nowhere.

The three of them had been lying on the rec, sharp ends of dried grass pricking at their bare arms and legs. Hours they had been messing around here, Bean and Smith's brains slowly addling in the heat.

"The saint." Bean, head shaped like a bean, arse producing shit-awful farts, had been licking along the length of a Rizla, sealing it up before picking a stray strand of tobacco out of the end, like he'd been making roll-ups for months not just the last few hours. Fifteen-year-olds in a park with their first bag of baccy. Pathetic really.

Any minute now they would get onto the gaylord thing again. Francis should have told them to fuck off straight up, not encouraged them. Instead he had laughed and said:

"Are we back in that shit hole, or something?" and he had flicked his thumb towards their old school.

Over there, in the playground just beyond this hedge and chain link fence that formed the barrier between the school and rec, Bean and Smith had taunted him about his bloody stupid, 'it was good enough for your grandfather' name. Now, four years on, bored in the park on a hot summer's day, and the dickheads were at it again.

"Oooo." Bean had blown smoke straight at Francis, pouted his mouth and let his wrist go limp, roll-up dangling. "Get her, St Francis the virgin."

"Yeah, right." Francis stood.

"Fancy some do you?" Bean passed the roll-up to Smith.

"What the fuck are you talking about?" Francis shoved his hands into his pockets, kicked out the sweaty creases in the knees of his shorts.

"This mate." Smith held out the roll-up. "What did you think we meant? A bit of arse?"

"That what you thought?" Bean set in too. "If we were asking you if you wanted a bit of batty boy bum?"

"Give me the cigarette." Francis held out his hand.

"Nah," Smith said and passed it back to Bean.

And they had both looked up at him from where, five minutes earlier, they had all been lying together contentedly, Bean with his arm crooked behind his head, roll-up drooping off his lip like it belonged there, Smith resting up on his elbow.

"Batty boy?" Smith repeated.

"Fuck off," Francis had shouted. "The pair of you, just fuck off."

And he had legged it across the rec, down the path to here, this gap in the hedge of his old primary school, where he now cowers like a stupid six-year-old.

Perhaps he should have told them right there and then. Perhaps he should have said that he had proof that being called Francis didn't make him fucking gay.

"Wankers." Francis spits out a piece of leaf and looks once more at the swimming pool glittering away, empty. The hedge is thin enough here. All he has to do is tug the fencing up and slip underneath. He can already imagine the sharp, cold water, the silent glugging in his ears.

"Oh Fraaaaan."

The cry is getting weaker, less distinct. They're pissing off. He eases his elbows out as far as he can, getting some air into his sodden armpits, and tugs at the bottom of the fence, bending it back as best he can. They'll be trying his mobile now, texting him, 'Arse' or fuck knew what. At home his phone, tucked away at the back of his wardrobe where no one can see or hear it, will be blinking away, message after message after message. All those messages he had come out today to avoid. All those missed calls from Steph.

A month ago she had stood before him, just over there in the trees behind the rec, her head to one side, forehead creased.

"Can you hear that?" she had asked him.

"What?" he said even though he already knew what she was starting on about. She'd been talking like this for months now.

"That noise."

"No," he had shaken his head. There was no noise, just her, and him, in the trees.

"A child crying?"

"There's no child, Steph."

"You can hear it."

"I can't. Honest. There's no noise."

"No noise." She had said that more quietly. "A baby. Are you sure?"

"Yeah. There's nothing. Honest."

She was picking at her fraying nails. *Click, click.*

"I'm going mad," she said.

"No, you're not."

"I am. I really am. I hear things. Like that baby. It's still crying, Francis."

"There's no baby."

She cupped her hands over her ears, eyes searching for the source of the sound.

"I hear things being said about me," she said. "Whispers. They tell me, tell me…"

"What do they tell you, Steph?"

"I need help, Francis."

He had shrugged. He didn't know.

"Hold me." She was crying. "Please."

So he held her, tighter than tight, her rapid breathing jarring against his chest. And then, somehow, he was kissing the salt from her cheeks, and her neck, and his hand was feeling the cool, bare skin of her back until they were lying together on the compacted mud beneath the trees, a root digging into his side, and she was all over him.

"You can make the voices go away," she had whispered as she slid her hand inside the front of his jeans, his face now as wet as hers.

"I can't."

"For a few minutes. Make them go."

"I really can't."

"Please, Francis."

He isn't gay. Francis knows that, and he could tell Bean and Smith that too, except he can't, because the proof is schizo Steph, and he should never have gone there, not however much he wanted to show those two, not however much she had begged him, never, because now whatever her problem is, it's his problem too and there is nothing he can do about it.

The ends of the wire dig into his back as he snakes under the fence, not caring if he gets cut. And then the water is there right in front of him, flickering at him, just like the light on his phone. Only this one is calling, 'Come in,' whereas the one on his phone yells, 'Help! Help! Help! Help!'

He tugs his shirt off over his head one-handed, dries his armpits and chest with it before throwing it onto the ground. He unbuttons his shorts, steps out of them and dives into the pool. And here, in the water where he and Bean and Smith had tottered in armbands on tippy-toes, where they had filled their eyes with tits swelling against Lycra and giggled. Here he too can hear voices, the voice of his mother asking what's wrong with him and why doesn't he put that bloody phone down, the voices of Bean and Smith asking if he wants arse, and Steph's tiny, tiny voice dying away as he sinks to the bottom.

Superstitions

Ffion raises her head from the pavement, merely as a matter of experiment. The brain is a smart device, Ffion knows that, smart in that whether she lies with her head on the side, parallel with the flagstone, or slightly raised, as it is now, at what might possibly be thirty degrees from the horizontal, she perceives the world to be orientated the same way. The reality of Ffion's perception is that the lamp posts in Fishers Way continue to point straight upwards, as does the step ladder above her and indeed the cat, who remains sitting obediently upright in its box, its black nose resting against the hole she cut for it to look out of.

"Yo," Ffion says, laying her cheek back on the pavement; the brain certainly is a smart device.

The other thing that Ffion has observed, about life and about nature, as she lies here, is that gravity sure is a major force. Quite how gravity works, Ffion is uncertain. She can describe how any two lumps of matter attract each other with a force directly proportional to the product of their masses and inversely proportional to the distance between them, and she can come up with an absolute measure of that force for any two bundles of particles, including her current attraction to the cat, given that she knows his or her weight. Oh yes, she can provide an objective measure for the gravitational pull between her and that cat, easy peasy. But what exactly is this compelling attraction between two bodies, and how does it work at a distance? Yes, that is the question she should really be considering. What on earth is gravity? Such a basic question.

Time to ponder. Ffion has time to ponder, and to lie, and to experiment with her visual perception of the street that she normally hurries along on her way to work at the university without giving it much of a second glance. All these things Ffion has time for right now.

A car turns the corner, then revs as it approaches the long straight, parallel with her position on the pavement outside her house. Unnecessary consumption of fuel, Ffion thinks. Gentle on the gas. Carbon footprint and all that. And, as if to obey her, the car slows as it passes, then accelerates away.

Her stars said that she should not venture out today. According to the advice for Leo she should stay in and adopt a more flexible attitude, the result of which will be that things will work out magically. Quite how the two actions of staying in and adopting a more flexible attitude hang together, Ffion isn't sure. Perhaps that was why Celeste the Psychic had needed to add a phone number after her advice.

Now, if Ffion were to assume that birth rates were evenly distributed across the year, probably an incorrect assumption but one that she will stick with for the purposes of her current deliberations, then a twelfth of the population would be covered by Celeste's edict to stay in, and if they all obeyed that advice, what would happen to the economy? Hospitals would shut, children and teachers would be forced to play hooky, and by the time the evening ended, there would be enough magically worked out unspecified things in the country to fill a rainbow. Tempting as it had been to engage in a live consultation with one of Celeste's team of astrologers, in order to define the abstract terms 'flexible attitude', 'things' and 'magically', Ffion had decided on her current alternative approach.

The cat mews. Ffion stretches out, feeling the gaps in between the paving slabs with her toes. Another car turns the corner into the street. That's two cars in five minutes. She wishes she had kept an accurate count of the cars that have passed in the hour she has been here so she could assess the relative rates of bike and car usage along Fishers Way at 9pm on a Friday evening. The car slows, stops, then reverses.

"You OK?"

"Fine," Ffion replies.

"Need an ambulance or anything?"

"No."

"You'll get cold."

And that is true enough, in some ways. Certainly she will ultimately get cold, but she ate macaroni cheese before venturing out, the source of food energy which will keep her adequately heated for a while, despite the continuing flow of heat energy from the more warm her to the less warm atmosphere.

"Eventually, I will get cold," she says, knowing that someone, somewhere will have calculated the time it would take for her to drift off into hypothermia, given the prevailing weather conditions and the temperature of the ground. She gives some thought to what shape that graph of her declining body temperature would take. Does the body maintain its temperature for a certain time and then drop suddenly? Is sixty-two minutes on a side street on an average evening in May, temperature 10 degrees Celsius, long enough? The Nazis had carried out experiments dropping Jews into vats of freezing water and monitoring their body temperature. Moral issue: should those experimental results be used to design safety suits for people falling into the North Sea, given that they were obtained through torture and denial of humanity? Should some sort of positive come out of such cruelty or should those measurements be destroyed in recognition of the abominable suffering caused?

Oh dear, this is becoming hard. Should she be including philosophy here?

The car engine falls silent. A door clicks open, clunks shut.

"Are you injured?"

"No."

"Sick?"

"I'm very well, thank you."

The man sniffs. Ffion is tempted to lift her head again, take a proper look at this man, but now someone is trying to interact with her she finds her situation slightly embarrassing. The cat has retreated to the back of its box.

"Nice evening," the man observes.

"Average," Ffion responds, for in terms of temperature, cloud cover and precipitation it is no nicer nor nastier than should be expected for the time of year. In many ways the evening is not noteworthy at all.

"Are you mad?" he asks.

Ffion laughs. That is a great question. She certainly isn't mad, so she should say no. But wouldn't a mad person, by definition also say no, since if they said yes they would have a sane insight into their condition, which would negate a diagnosis of madness. For a moment Ffion considers the possible double negatives in this thought process before deciding that the logical conclusion of her argument must be that only a mad person would deny their madness.

"Yes," she replies thus demonstrating not only that she isn't mad but also that she has a keen sense of irony, which would be nice to have.

The feet back away. Nice shoes, sky-blue canvas baseball boots, not too shoddy, not too new. The cat's nose appears at the opening in the box.

"That your cat?"

"No," Ffion replies. Strictly speaking she should add that she has borrowed it, but she can see how that might be misconstrued in these circumstances, particularly as the man's voice has a certain calmness about it, an authority.

"I am looking after it," she decides to add to explain its presence.

"I'm thinking that you might have taken a tumble," the man says. "Knocked into that ladder there, or perhaps the cat wriggled in its box and sent you off balance and you fell."

"Oh, no," Ffion says. "That didn't happen."

"A rather unlikely set of occurrences, I agree," the man says.

He pokes his toe at the cat box, shifting it slightly. Then he says:

"When I see a cat in a box," he pauses. Perhaps she will look up at him, take a peek, "I always think of ..." He stops.

"Of what?" Ffion asks, her throat unusually tight, her heart rather more active than necessary, hoping the word Schrodinger might be voiced.

"Forget it. You're all right?"

"Yo, look at me. What could be wrong?"

Schrodinger's cat. Why hadn't Ffion revisited that whole excellent thought experiment as she lay here? She will give it some consideration now. A cat sealed in a box with a diabolical mechanism made up of a small amount of a radioactive substance and a phial of poison. If the radioactive substance decays, the phial shatters and the cat is killed. The Copenhagen interpretation of quantum theory implies that after a while the cat in the box is simultaneously both alive and dead. Mad. Brilliant. The *reductio ad absurdum* of quantum physics. Ffion could happily spend quite a bit of time discussing that with the right person.

The feet step away, swish, swish.

Sod it. She has completed her task. She sits up, her back stiff from the stone pavement.

"Hey," she calls. "Thanks for stopping."

The man raises his hand, opens the car door. Then without getting in shuts it again and walks back towards her.

"What are you doing?" he asks.

"Experimenting."

He looks at the cat and the ladder.

"On what?"

Now Ffion has been asked the question, she wonders why she is doing this? An empty evening, an irritation with Celeste the Psychic, and an unsettling urge for some magic in her life don't seem very compelling reasons any longer. Sod it, he has asked.

"Friday the thirteenth," she explains. "Walking under a ladder, touching the cracks in the pavement, being out against an astrologer's advice, a black cat. I just wanted to prove that superstitions are bollocks."

The man stands for a while.

"So, what is your hypothesis?" he asks.

Her hypothesis? Even thinking about voicing it feels stupid.

"You really want to know?"

The man flicks his hands as if to indicate that she doesn't know what she is talking about.

"OK," Ffion says, "I'll tell you what my hypothesis is. To prove that being superstitious is ridiculous, I set the hypothesis of 'If I breach at least five superstitions then I will meet the man of my dreams'."

Why she had set meeting the man of her dreams as her experimental outcome, Ffion isn't sure. Men had never been much of a feature in Ffion's life, not even in her dreams. Not because of any particular aversion on her part, simply that it appears that her rigorously analytical approach to life isn't something that the men she meets find attractive in a woman.

"Stupid, hey?" she adds.

"Yeah, really stupid," the man says. "Unscientific too."

The cat mews again. Ffion probably shouldn't have picked a strange cat off the street and put it in a box.

"It lacks a quantitatively measurable outcome and as such is un-provable," he says.

"I know," Ffion stands up, rather stiffer than she had expected, and folds the step ladder.

She had pondered over defining the man of her dreams in absolute terms. A degree might be one thing on the list, but how much did that really matter. And then certain measurable criteria for the way he looked, height, eye colour and so forth. Someone who would talk and listen to her, perhaps, but that lacked the specificity of duration and amount of verbal interaction. So she had abandoned all that and decided that should such a situation arise, she would set her measurables based on whatever experience came her way.

"Still, eh," she adds.

She lifts the step ladder onto her shoulder.

"What about the cat?" the man asks.

"I guess we can let it go now," Ffion says.

The man bends down.

"But," he says before lifting the lid, "when I open it, will the cat be dead or alive?"

It is now that Ffion decides that canvas shoes will have to be included in her list of measurables for the man of her dreams. Yes, sky-blue canvas baseball boots. Those are certainly a good start.

Petrification

The night-troll children were fishing down by the lake, dragging in net after net of salmon. So entranced were they by their bountiful haul that they forgot to keep an eye on the night sky. As the first glimmers of dawn infused the darkness, the mother troll rushed out of her cave to call her children to safety, only to discover them petrified. While she stared in shock, the morning light sloped on up the hill to strike her and she became petrified too.

So there they are, lumps of stone, one large boulder at the top gazing down at the smaller ones stuck forever on the shore of Lake Ugly.

We were told that story on the first day when we had yet to learn each other's names.

Volcanically heated pool at Landmannaglaugar, 6th September 2014

She stands in her swimming costume, water up to mid-thigh, her hand raised as though shielding her eyes from the sun. Except I don't remember the sun shining. I remember the wind later that night, strong enough to rattle the hut's corrugated iron roof as we lay in columns in our sleeping bags, surrounded by gentle breaths and ferocious snores. And I remember the snow the following morning that drove into our ears and nostrils as we trudged our way through the rhyolite mountains, the most dramatic scenery in Iceland, had we been able to see it through the blizzard.

Her face is dark beneath the shadow of her hand so that if this were the only photo I had of her, I would have nothing to remind me of her features. Perhaps she is waving. At me? At the group admiring the first person brave enough to get into the volcanic pool?

"Come on you lot," she is saying. "It's beautiful in here."

I hadn't expected the unevenness of the water's heat or the softness of the mud which moulded itself round my weary feet.

That first night she slept three people away from me. I noticed where she lay and as I said good night to everyone in general, I was really only saying good night to her.

View down from the top of a small volcano, 7th September 2014

The moss covering the sides of the volcano is ancient, grown from seeds blown on the wind from Europe. It takes for ever to re-form if disturbed, so it is important to step carefully.

From up here, the landscape is tri-coloured, green, black and grey moss and lava. But at its moment of creation, the valley must have crackled and blazed orange and red, and sulphur must have poisoned this untainted air.

Way below, in the group of ten or so red and blue coated people, she stands, except I cannot tell which one she is in this photo. I had hoped she would climb too, rather than stay all the way down there in the tired-leg crowd. I hadn't wanted to ask, or make it obvious that it was her company I enjoyed above the others'. It was only our second day.

But she is down there, and I am up here, and I must have lingered long enough to take this photo before I trod my delicate way back down.

Ice cave, 8th September 2014

She is bent over, her backpack hard against the cave's blue roof, stuck like a tortoise.

"Do you think there are any trolls in here, Emma?" she is calling.

Perhaps she didn't use those precise words, but she used my name; she knew it by then, and I knew hers.

"Yeah." I laughed. I know I laughed because even in the photo she is comical.

"Ahh!" She struggles, trapped in an ice cave with trolls.

"Don't worry," I call. "The elves will rescue you."

Elf church, 8th September 2014

Elves are peaceful beings, as long as they are treated with respect. They resemble small humans and are the light on trees and flowers; that better side of nature where feet aren't frozen with glacial water and wind shards don't penetrate waterproof coats. And they have a church where they marry, this one; a rock formation with a roof like an elf's hat.

Here in Iceland you should be kind to strangers. You never know who, or what they might be.

We had been strangers.

In the hut at Hvanngil that night, I slept next to her. A room for twelve with three sets of double bunk-beds. When the couples and men had been matched up, she and I were the only two left. Perhaps I dreamt of the elf church and romance that night. I don't remember. But I do remember her lose arm across my chest, her breath on my cheek.

On the plateau at Heljarkambur after the scary climb, 9th September 2014

She cried and held onto the chain attached to the side of the hill.

"You're all right," I said.

She didn't believe me.

"Nothing's going to happen."

Volcanic scree slithered beneath her feet. The earth was untrustworthy. I had lied, something could very well happen.

"One small step at a time."

I had never seen anyone actually frozen with fear before.

"You can do it."

She shook her head, eyes shut tight.

"One tiny step."

75

Behind us someone was crying and someone else was telling them just to take one small step.

"Try it."

I put my hand over hers and eased the fingers off the chain. She attached herself to me, jarring me backwards, but I didn't mind if we fell down the slope together. I would have gone anywhere with her.

"That's it. And another. Good."

Every movement was made awkward by the stiff trembling in her legs.

"Not far now."

Twenty metres could have been the other side of the world for all the courage she had to find within her to cover the distance.

"No, don't look down, just look at the chain in front of you. It's not going anywhere."

When the chain ended, she crawled onto the plateau, grasping hold of the ground and sobbing:

"You saved my life."

In the photo, this one taken on the plateau only a few minutes after the scary climb, she glows with the ecstasy of survival.

Crossing a river near Thorsmork, 10th September 2014

Our boots are tied round our necks and our trousers rolled up as we wade, facing slightly upstream, holding onto a guide rope. Someone in blue with a cream hat, whose name I don't remember now, is mid-stream. A queue has formed.

She sought me out, moving among the group to find me, not for anything in particular, just to walk with me and talk. Egg and chips, we decided, that would be our first meal back in the world of running hot water and showers, away from this surreal place of black sand and blue ice lakes, where one is encouraged to believe in the fabulous.

She held my hand as we walked and, once we had crossed the river, she steadied herself on my arm to dry her feet with her socks, first one, then the other. I didn't get a photo of her boots going back on, I was too busy feeling the weight of her grip on my wrist.

Walk past the waterfalls to Skogar, 11ᵗʰ September 2014

Eleven waterfalls, one after the other, after the other, until the river flings itself over a sixty-metre-high cliff. Water racing down, losing energy with every fall, collapsing, inevitably, into the uniform sea.

How many waterfalls can you see in one afternoon and keep saying *ahhh* at? Believe me, it is somewhere less than eleven.

"I can't look at them anymore," she says, striding ahead. "My eyes are all full up of waterfalls."

This is our last day of walking and, whether she looks or not, the waterfalls matter, because we are passing each one of them together, losing energy with every step, descending, inevitably, back to normality, together.

Geysir, 12ᵗʰ September 2014

There is a stone engraved with 'GEYSIR' in the foreground, just in case I forget where we are. Behind the stone, water vapour trails rise out of the earth. Next to it eight people have lined up to pose for this photo.

We are sightseeing on the way to the airport. In less than six hours we will part at Gatwick and holiday friendships will become a list of email addresses, scrunched somewhere in a drawer, and these photographs.

Could we ever be anything other than strangers who had been kind to each other? Perhaps I should have left the question unthought and contented myself with these photos, as I am now, grateful for what had been. But this was the world where fantasy and reality were one.

A steaming, blue-grey dome is caught the moment before it re-cedes. We are being taunted by a bubble of water building up its breath, preparing to explode, or not. And as we wait, untouching, even though we have touched so often and are close enough now to touch again, I ask:

"Shall we keep in contact?"

"Could do," she replies.

"That'd be great. Maybe we could meet up."

"Sure."

The dome rises to a metre high.

"We could go walking or something. Or perhaps another holiday like this one?"

I reach out and touch her arm.

"You know I'm not gay," she says.

The water has slunk back into its black hole.

"I know," I say. "Do you think I didn't know that?"

"I did wonder," she says.

"You needn't have wondered," I say. "I knew."

The water re-emerges in a rush.

"If you'd prefer not to meet," I say. "That's fine too."

She doesn't answer. She is watching the geyser.

That picture of the boiling water spouting thirty metres into the air remains snapped on my retina alone. I was unable to hold my camera. My hands and heart had turned to stone.

Strands

This bedroom has a brown carpet. It has a bed with blankets which smell musty and a chest of drawers with a half-peeled sticker of Donny Osmond on. Tommy is to make himself at home in this room. He sits on the bed and listens. Downstairs, Sheila is clanking a pan in the kitchen. He pulls his *Adidas* bag onto his lap and waits.

Dinner, they call it, and it is a pork chop, a big thick one, with mashed potatoes and cabbage. Tommy eats it all, picks up the bone too. And then he sees that they have cut the fat off their chops, left it on the side. His fat is eaten. He wants to eat theirs as well, almost spears it off their plates. He waits for them to tell him off for eating his fat. They don't, they just scrape theirs into the bin.

It's bedtime and Tommy has a bath with bubbles in. Sheila says his hair needs washing and that she'll never do it properly if he keeps his hands clasped tight to his head like that. So he closes his eyes and holds the hand without the plaster cast over his willy. She tuts, rubs hard and says: "Oh, sorry, did I push that bruise? Did it hurt?"

"No," Tommy says. Pushing a bruise isn't hurting.

Tommy lies with his bag beside him that night, waiting.

Barbara comes round to see him in that house, takes him up to the room with the brown carpet and tells him that being there isn't permanent. He should pack. She has a green Volkswagen Beetle with the engine in the back so his *Adidas* bag goes in the boot at the front. Sheila wipes her eyes and Barbara says to say goodbye and thank you. She tells him to put his seatbelt on. It pulls all the way out, zips back in again. Out and in.

"Just put it on," Barbara says at the street corner.

This bedroom has a green carpet with a worn patch by the door. It has bunk beds, not for sharing with anyone though; he has to have his own room because of shouting in the night. It has a wardrobe, white with gold handles. Karen tells him to unpack. He says he doesn't want to unpack. She says she'll help.

Michael is Karen's son, who is the same age as Tommy. Susie is the baby with wispy hair. Michael dissects mouse bones out of an owl pellet with a knife and tweezers. He lets Tommy watch but not touch, and then not watch either. Tommy takes the knife from Michael's room, tries it out on lumps of mud in the garden, hides it in the wardrobe in his room and waits.

Big Michael ruffles Little Michael's head when he gets home from work. They eat beans and vegetables with rice because eating meat is killing.

The plaster cast is cut off Tommy's itchy arm. He thinks he might keep it, but they put it in the bin at the hospital. Sheila had written her name in purple on that plaster cast.

"You'll be back to playing football again," the doctor says.

Susie doesn't squeak when he pulls one of the hairs out of her head, and then another. She just carries on staring at him as though she doesn't feel anything. He gathers all the strands together and sits on his *Adidas* bag in the wardrobe with the knife, and the hair, and the door shut.

This room he shares with five other boys. It has no carpet, just blue lino with a deep scratch mark that has turned black. Six beds, each with a drawer underneath. Barbara says *no more foster homes* because of the broken wardrobe and the yelling. She doesn't say anything about Susie, she just says goodbye and passes him on to Barry. Tommy sits on his bed, imagining he is Little Michael with an owl's pellet.

Tommy can stop worrying now, that's what Barry tells him. He is staying here where he is safe, where his mum and step-dad can't find him. Honest. Tommy can settle down and be a boy again. And he doesn't need to call out at night any longer. Really. He can stop that, right now.

Tommy takes his shirts from his *Adidas* bag, refolding them so they pile exactly on top of each other, like Karen did, before he places them in the drawer.

This flat has a newly-fitted brown carpet that smells of clean dust and rubber. Tom goes to the *Mind* shop to buy something to make the place his own. The woman behind the counter dings the till open, slams it shut, hands him his cow creamer wrapped in newspaper.

"You don't often see these nowadays," she says.

Back in his flat Tom places the cow creamer on the windowsill and thinks about the shop woman with the broken nail on her index finger, her unmade-up face and lopsided hair. He returns and asks her name.

"Janey," she says. "It's Janey."

He tells her his is Michael.

"You look like a Michael," Janey says.

He doesn't leave. Instead he pretends to examine the row of CDs and the rail of shirts. He picks up a pair of shoes.

"Do you want to buy those?" Janey asks.

"These?"

"Yes."

"No."

He puts the shoes back on the shelf, neatly lined up, before returning to the counter.

"How's the cow creamer?" she asks.

"Good," he says. Then he asks, "Janey, will you go out with me?"

"Why did you tell me you were called Michael?" Janey shouts.

They have been together for three months and Tom has never heard her raise her voice before. He cups invisible hands over his ears and thinks about the bag he keeps under his bed containing a toothbrush and shirt and pants.

"Why?" she repeats.

"I knew someone called Michael once," he tells her.

"And I knew someone called Venetia. I didn't tell you my name was Venetia, did I? You're asking a lot expecting me to trust you when I've been calling you by the wrong name all this time. That's a betrayal, Mike, Tom. A betrayal. I don't know who you are any longer. Why did you do it?"

"I liked you," he says. "I wanted you to like me."

"By using the name of someone you knew once? You're twenty, Mi-, Tom, not eight."

"I thought you'd like him more than me."

"Maybe I would, but you're not him. You're you. I like you."

Janey wants to have a baby, but Tom cannot bear the thought of Janey's baby ending up with a father like him. Someone who tugs a baby's hair. Someone malign. He starts crying in the night, thrashing around.

"Who's Susie?" Janey demands in the morning.

"Susie?"

"You're seeing someone else, aren't you?"

"No."

"That's why you don't want to have a baby with me. I knew I should never have trusted you."

Janey lets it drop. Janey gets pregnant. Tom cries, not tears of happiness or delight, but gut-crunching, grief-stricken tears that make Janey cry too.

"You'll get used to the idea," she says. "When our baby's born you'll love it as much as I do." She places his hand on her stomach. He pulls away.

Tom needs to apologise before he leaves for good. He takes the packed bag from under his bed and, even though Karen and Michael probably won't live in the same house any longer, he knocks on their door. The door opens to reveal a wooden floor, golden and long. He doesn't remember how it was before. Carpet?

"Hello." He transfers the bag to his other hand and waits for the door to be shut in his face.

"Hello?" Karen is shorter and her hair is solid black now with no fringe. She rests a hand on her hip. She doesn't know who he is. He shouldn't have come.

"It's Tom," he says. "Tommy." No one has called him Tommy for years. "I stayed with you once, about ten years ago? For a few months maybe?"

"Of course, Tommy," she says as though nothing ever happened. "Come on in."

The house is smaller and the walls are yellow, not covered in wallpaper with big orange flowers.

"How are you, Tommy?" she asks.

"Fine, thanks. And you?"

"Good."

The kitchen table is the same, and the blue striped mugs - he had forgotten those. Karen fills the kettle as though she's asked him to stay for a cuppa, as though he's agreed.

"Are you working?" She pops two tea bags into the pot.

"I'm a gardener."

"Now that doesn't surprise me. You were always out in the garden."

Tom doesn't remember that.

"You ate beans," he says.

"You picked them out." She laughs.

"Did I?" he says. "I get confused."

"Who wouldn't after what you went through. Such a muddled time."

The kettle clicks off.

"How's Michael?" Tom asks.

"He's fine. Both Michaels are fine. Little Michael lives in Edinburgh now with his wife. Not so little anymore."

She takes two of the stripy mugs, gets a container of milk from the fridge.

"And Susie?" He closes his eyes to shut out the sound of the fading siren and rid his fingers of the feel of the soft, spidery hair.

"Living with her boyfriend."

"She's OK?"

"OK?" Karen asks as though she never carried Susie into the ambulance, as though Barbara never arrived to take him to the home.

"After the hospital? Her hair and everything?"

"Hair?" Karen pours the tea slowly. "Nothing to do with her hair, poor little mite. Constipation. Have you been worrying about her all this time?"

"Must have been."

"They should have told you she was OK."

Nothing to do with Susie's hair. Not her head. The fridge hums. Tom holds his mug between his hands and remembers hot chocolate next to a bonfire, he remembers Big Michael handing him a sparkler, he remembers playing flaming swords with Little Michael and Susie giggling as he clutched his hand to an imaginary wound and fell to the ground. He remembers Karen rubbing the mud from his back and then just rubbing to keep him warm. He remembers Big Michael ruffling his hair. He checks his watch. Janey will be home from working at the shop now. She'll be sitting in the flat with the unopened packs of sleep suits and the musical mobile with sheep on, wondering why he's not there to help her pack her hospital bag.

"My girlfriend's expecting a baby." He wasn't going to tell Karen that, but now, somehow, Tom doesn't like the thought of Janey sitting there, waiting while her baby's father is goodness knows where. He doesn't like it at all.

"That's fabulous news."

"I'd best get back to her." He puts down his half-finished tea. At the front door he turns. "I nearly forgot." He removes the cow creamer from his bag.

"How lovely," Karen says.

"For you. Sort of an apology."

"An apology?" Karen says. "Nothing to apologise for, you daft thing."

"And to say thanks."

"That's kind." Karen takes it. "Now, you look after that girlfriend of yours."

Tom thinks of Janey in the shop before she was his girlfriend, the nails, the stray loop of hair.

"Of course," he says.

"You'll make a great dad."

"You think so?"

"Yeah, I think so."

"Thanks," he says.

He'll go straight back home now and empty his bag. He'll help Janey pack it with the baby things, all neatly piled. He'll pat her tummy and not worry so much about harming the baby's fluffy head. And he'll touch Janey's hair. Ruffle it maybe, then stroke the strands back into place.

Snow Blindness

Greg stands at the top of the red run, the wind blowing the snow up the slope ahead of him, a curtain of shocking cold steam beating against his face. All he can hear is the muted clatter of the chairlift behind him. Two boarders carve past, but other than them no one is riding up on the lift. Most people are down in the valley eschewing this morning's bitterly cold mountains.

He points his skis downhill and sets off into the white-out, the murky piste posts that mark the relative safety of the slope thickening and fading as the clouds pass. In the absence of any view or sound to distract him, he focuses fully on his body, skiing by the feel through his feet exactly as Marie-Laure had instructed him during his lessons.

"Hips forward," she had said. "In the love position. You must feel, Greg, or your skiing is bad."

He had loved her English with its jaunty edge, literally translated from the French, he presumed. And her lipstick smile, he had loved that too. Now, on his own on the invisible slope, he thrusts his hips forward as he had done for Marie-Laure, smiling at the memory of her laugh, a moment of shared amusement defying their language boundaries.

He has no idea how fast he is moving in this sensory-deprived world. Here he is insulated from everything and everybody, alone, and on this unfamiliar run, not knowing where the edge of the piste is and what lies beyond. A plummet into a snow-filled ditch? A buffeting fall through pines into the valley?

"Don't go out today," April had said. It was the way she had spoken that had stopped his dithering and spurred him on to getting dressed. He knew he couldn't spend today with her.

"I'm here to ski," he replied, pulling on his thermal top.

"For God's sake." April lay in their hotel bed, the duvet up round her neck, the warmth of their night captured next to her night-dressed, scarred body. "You don't have to go out every day, you know. The weather's atrocious."

89

"It can't be that bad if the lifts are open." He searched for socks, not wanting to look at her. "It might be better up the mountain."

"It won't be."

Somehow April knew this, just as surely as any local would have known the intricate details of the weather system in the valley. Based on what? The tiny bit of the street she could observe through the small gap in the curtain?

"Anyway, you can't ski alone," she added.

"You coming then?" he asked.

"No."

She hadn't wanted to be on this holiday in the first place, just hadn't wanted him to come alone.

"See you later." He gathered his goggles and gloves together.

"Why are you doing this?" April's voice was lower now, infused with the gravity she had recently adopted to show how monumental her insight into life had become. Was she implying the normal, that he was wasting his life while she was struggling for hers? Or was she saying something different this morning?

She sat up and rustled the bed clothes demurely around her shoulders, as though he might be a stranger in her room come to tidy it, not her lover of three years. He turned his back fully on her and shrugged.

"You're stupid," she decreed.

Greg paused, not thinking about what she had said but about her certainty.

"Bye," he had said and he clicked the door shut behind him.

The fog melts and he sees a piste post, two, now three, the last one down a steep slope. He picks up speed, short tight turns, weight forward, the unbashed snow piling up on top of his boots as he adopts the love position.

Shit! What was that? A sudden drop, yet he is still upright, still ploughing on.

Squandering his life is what April persistently accuses him of nowadays. Nights out with work colleagues, or the occasional cigarette, or watching something she doesn't enjoy on the TV, indeed anything that she would prefer not to do herself, is squandering precious moments. Yet, down in the hotel room, April has herself warmly wrapped in a duvet to protect what remains of her, obsessing over whether the next check-up will be clear, retreating from the world to live in total safety all those extra minutes, months or years gifted her by expert doctors.

Yesterday afternoon, after his third and final skiing lesson, Marie-Laure had given him her card. She had said to give her a call if he wanted any more lessons.

"Lessons on the love position?" he had asked, joking in the way they had joked for the past two afternoons.

Marie-Laure's response had been what? A dismissive shrug? A *come on* signal? How was he to know, he was a man and body language a mysterious form of communication only interpretable by women. Yet this didn't stop April chastising him when he got one of her sighs or a gesture wrong. He couldn't comment on her inconsistency though. That wouldn't be fair.

His thighs burn and despite the blasts of alpine air he is warming beneath his four layers. He digs in his downhill ski, his legs juddering to a halt, and as he does so he falls into the powder snow.

The laugh comes from the middle of his belly, a proper kid's chuckle. How ridiculous is this? He has been skiing down goodness knows what and yet has only fallen now he has stopped. Despite the cold he continues to lie, allowing the pillow of snow to frost his face, imagining Marie-Laure laughing while poking at him with her ski pole.

Last night he had told April he was going out to mooch round the town.

"Get a beer, you mean," she had said in her 'squandering life' way.

"Probably," he said, deciding it was easier to admit to that than anything else. "You want to come?" He added just to show quite how innocent his outing was going to be.

"I think I'll rest," April replied.

The phone conversation with Marie-Laure had been awkward, the language differences seeming to multiply when he couldn't see her face, the couple of hours they had spent apart making them strangers again.

"You take another lesson?" Marie-Laure asked. Was she smiling as she spoke? Greg had no idea.

Momentarily he thought about answering yes, that would be good, another lesson was exactly what he needed, perhaps concentrating on his off-piste technique. A gentle double-entendre, should she choose to pick up on it. But he didn't know whether her grasp of English would be up to understanding his meaning. He also didn't know whether another moment like this would ever come along for him, not now that he understood the future was not infinite, that mortality might strike at the most unexpected time, that he could die tomorrow.

"No," he had replied. "Not another lesson. I wondered if you would like a drink with me, to say thank you, for the lessons?" Those last words had been tagged on to make him sound reasonable, not a man out to snare his pretty, funny ski instructor who probably received twenty such offers a week. Christ, he didn't even know whether she was married or had a boyfriend, but in three days' time he would be back home locked in the endless cycle of people asking how April was getting on and tonight he didn't have to be.

"Teaching skiing is my job. I don't need a drink to say thank you," Marie-Laure replied.

"No problem," Greg responded. And that was it, he supposed. Valiant, foolhardy approach made and rebuffed. But she hadn't rushed in with a goodbye to end the call. She had left the line open, blank for a whole hopeful, beckoning few seconds.

"Just an idea." Greg filled the silence. "That was all."

Still Marie-Laure didn't hang up. Or maybe she wasn't listening any longer. Perhaps she had been distracted by something on the TV he could hear in the background. At this point he should have said thanks, or goodbye, instead he said, "I enjoyed our time together."

And she replied, "Me too. OK, so we have a drink."

"Now?" Greg asked wondering whether he could get away with not returning to the hotel for a few hours. April would be reading, no doubt, resting against the danger of any fatigue that might come her way.

"Yes, now if you like," Marie-Laure replied.

And so they had met, and they had drunk *Jagerbombs* until Greg had noticed the time.

April had stirred when he had entered the hotel room early this morning. He had paused his step, held his breath, until he heard no further movement. For what reason, he wasn't sure. He had been out drinking, exactly as he had told her. Après ski and all that. He slipped silently into bed, keeping his cold body away from her so as not to disturb her.

"You all right, mate?" A skier swooshes up on him from out of nowhere.

Greg sits up from his snow bed.

"Yeah," he says, realising that the word had formed in his head far quicker than his mouth had been able to announce it. His reactions have become dulled.

"Fucking freezing," the skier says. "Calling it a day. Fucking waste of a lift pass." And he is off.

Greg gets to his feet, kicks the snow off his skis and starts on down. Since stopping, every turn aches and his legs feel clumsy, jarring on each powder drift. He rides the snow mounds; takes a deep breath to get the oxygen into his blood and round his body. Right, he is ready. He points his skis downhill to build up speed, but again when it comes to the turn his legs are awkward. Perhaps he will forget the turns. How fast can he get? The falling snow, uncompacted by either piste basher or skier, slows his progress, yet despite that there is now a consistent wind straight in his face. He is certainly moving, powering on. Slowly his body is clicking into sync. Wow, this is stupendous. Freedom, elation, flight.

When he had mentioned needing to get back to the hotel last night, Marie-Laure had asked him back to her place. He had gone with her, simple as that. How wondrous it had been to spend an hour with her, to have carefree sex with someone who wasn't scared of being touched or hurt. Someone who wanted him rather than tolerated him. Simple, straightforward sex with no duties or obligations, and at the end a mutually understood, 'Goodbye'. The very same word he had been preparing to deliver to April just before she had been diagnosed, before her illness and treatment and personality had become so intertwined that he couldn't be sure any longer which of the three he abhorred the most.

The cloud dissipates and below him he can clearly see the lift station. Two days ago, he would have caught the cable car to head back down into the valley to April. He would have apologised for going out and upsetting her by taking a risk with his life. He would have numbly held her, told her everything would be all right, as he has done for what seems like most of his life. Today, though, he allows himself to feel for the first time in two years. He fully embraces the love position and heads for the chairlift to take him back up the mountain. Today he is going to squander his life, spend every last moment of it. Christ, today he feels alive.

Tonight's Dream

Enter stage left. Consider the audience. Check one's hands. Move to centre stage with a hop and a skip, a whoop maybe. Then fling arms open, showering confetti, the mock rose-petal type, across the stage. Smile. This will be tonight's dream.

Enter stage left. Consider the audience. Check one's hands. Check one's hands again.

Enter stage. The auditorium is full, no spare seats in the Stalls, or the Royal Circle, or the Upper Circle. Check again. The auditorium lights are low, it's not easy to see. There. Stalls row M, or N perhaps, a seat tipped up. Someone has left. A trip to the toilet? That will be it. Check one's hands. Move to centre stage.

Enter stage. One's eyes are drawn to the Stalls, row N, N23 to be exact. The seat is tipped up. The ticket holder has not yet arrived. On their way here, no doubt, delayed somewhere. Check one's hands are clean, thoroughly clean, washed, dried and washed again, so as not to taint the confetti in one's pockets. The seats to both sides of N23 are occupied, one by a man, his elbow on the communal arm rest, the other by a girl, no, a young woman, but so slight she could be a girl. She sits upright as though balancing a book on her head, her left hand clutching her ponytail at the back of her head.

The stage. The almost-full auditorium. The empty seat. Check one's hands. A fleck of brown. Mud perhaps, but just a fleck, on the end of the forefinger of the right hand. The thumb nail pick, picks. The mud needs to be gone. Pick.

Tickets N22 and N23 were bought as a pair. A young woman reserved them, a teenager with a tight-back ponytail.

"Two tickets for Journey's End, please," she said. "The Thursday evening performance. In the Upper Circle, please."

She held her purse in both hands upright on the counter. The man in the box office pulled round a monitor and tapped away.

"We only have Stalls tickets left for that night." He glanced up at her.

"Only Stalls? How much are they?" the young woman asked.

"Sixty-eight pounds for the two. And actually," he clicked away at the keyboard, eyes scanning he screen, "there's only the one pair in the Stalls. Otherwise it's just a few odd seats on their own here and there. You wanted Upper Circle, did you?"

"Yes."

"Would you like me to see if there's anything for another evening?"

"No. It needs to be Thursday." The girl reached back for her ponytail and held it tight. "Sixty-eight pounds?" she checked.

"Yes."

She let go of her hair, glanced at her purse.

"OK," she said.

The almost-full auditorium with the empty seat, and on the stage three men in uniform sit at a trestle table while bass notes vibrate the theatre walls. *Kaboom, crash.* They speak of dispatches being sent up the line, of old school days. They drink and a young lad, full of excitement and derring-do, is having his spirits crushed by a former idol who has grown weary and cynical. A shell explodes and the audience knows that for these men on stage there is no future, that this story is full of dramatic irony. It is hopeless.

"Oh, darling, what a nice idea," the young woman's mother said.

"You said you studied it at school."

"I did. That's right. Long time ago now."

"Not that long, Mum."

"Seems like an age."

"We can get a taxi there."

"A taxi?"

"Travel in style. Better than the bus."

"That'll be nice, darling."

The safety curtain falls. The audience claps. Lights up in the auditorium and couples exit leaving coats crumpled on chairs and tonight's newspaper crushed with plastic wine glasses on the floor beneath. Everyone has left apart from the woman in N22 who stays staring at the stage.

"I'll wear my purple dress, darling."

"That one suits you."

"My purple dress and black shoes."

"You'll look lovely, Mum."

"Thank you, darling."

Enter stage. The set remains as it was left after the second act - the enamel mug lies on its side, the flask hangs from the hook. Nothing has changed. Consider the audience. Check one's hands. Move to centre stage. Check one's hands again. The fleck of mud has moved, it has smudged down onto the palm. Wipe it off on the opposite palm, rub, rub. The mud will soil the confetti. Rub, rub. Apart from the tipped up seat in row N, the auditorium has refilled. Someone coughs. Someone cracks an ice cream spoon. A shh.

"Tonight, darling? Is it tonight?"

"Yes, Mum. It's your birthday, remember. Happy birthday."

"I hadn't put two and two together, that's all."

"The taxi's booked for quarter to seven. I told you that."

"You did."

"I'll help you dress when I get home from school."

"That'll be nice."

"Make sure you eat your lunch. It's on the tray in the kitchen."

"Don't fuss, darling."

"And we'll have tea when I get in. A birthday tea."

"Lovely."

"I've put a tea towel over your lunch, Mum. Make sure the dog doesn't go in there."

"He'll stay with me, won't you, Dennis."

99

"You will eat?"

"Of course."

The mud won't budge. Fingers pick, fingers scratch with satisfying pain. Harder and harder but all that happens is the mud spreads over the back of the hands, up the arms. One touches one's hair, grabs hold of the ponytail hanging down one's back, and in doing so dusts the forearm against the nose. And now this isn't mud at all, it's shit, stinking watery shit that runs over the top lip and seeps into the mouth, finding the gaps between one's teeth, pouring down one's throat.

"You didn't eat."

"I wasn't hungry, darling."

"You need to eat. You won't be up to the theatre tonight if you don't eat anything."

"Is it tonight?"

"Yes. I reminded you this morning. And you didn't put Dennis out."

"He didn't want to go."

"He needs to be put out, Mum. He's piddled in the hallway. I'll put him out now."

"He doesn't like going out."

Enter stage left. Consider the audience. Blink through the shit that's pouring down one's face. Place one's hands over one's groin and arse just in case anyone thinks one has shat oneself, that this whole stinking mess is one's own fault.

"Happy birthday to you, happy birthday to you, happy birthday dear Mu-um, happy birthday to you. Blow. Big breath. Shall I do it for you? There now, wish." The young woman angled the knife. "A big slice of cake for you."

"What about you, darling?"

"I'm OK, I had lunch at school."

"Are you sure? You're getting very skinny?"

"There you go." The young woman placed a slice of chocolate cake on a plate.

"Eat up and then we'll get you dressed."

"For what?"

"For the theatre."

"Is that tonight?"

"Yes, Mum. I did tell you."

"Oh, darling."

"What?"

"I'm not so sure."

"*Journey's End*. You studied it at school. You told me all about it. I've bought the tickets, booked a taxi."

"You are good."

"You'll feel better after cake."

Enter stage left. Consider the audience. The auditorium is full, completely full, every last seat occupied. Check one's hands, shiny clean, not a speck of dust. Move to centre stage with a hop and a skip, a whoop maybe. Then fling arms open, showering confetti, the circular, mock rose petal type, across the stage. Smile. This will be tonight's dream.

Shooting Waters

Aimar plays shooting waters with a bag with a tiny hole in the corner and a puddle swished up into it. He holds the top tight and squashes it, aiming the spray at his and Joram's plastic tent. The water bleeds down the side, little dribbles.

"Hey, Joram," he calls.

Surely Joram has heard the spurt of the water against the plastic. Surely he is crouching behind the black canvas which hangs over the doorway, giggling.

"Joram, you scoundrel."

Still no noise. Aimar stoops to scoop what's left of the puddle and, as he rises, his trousers come away from the string holding them up. The lady from Germany brought the trousers, just after the barbed wire had been laid across the roads and fields. She held them up against him, pushed her fingertips with the fabric into his sides as though it mattered that they reached half-way round him.

"Thank you," he said and whatever she replied he didn't understand so he looked away, not wanting to see if she was angry or sad. But she went on talking as though he were three instead of thirteen and that made him stare even harder at the police.

Aimar is taller now and thinner. The trousers don't stay up and, when he squats, they come away at the back so that he is forever holding the material to stop people looking. But that is fine, since the trousers are his and no one will mind as he was given them by one of the German ladies who came and went.

He reaches behind and hitches the waistband over the string.

"Joooooooraaam!" He lines up the corner of the bag again and removes his finger from the pin prick hole as he applies pressure with his elbow. This time he doesn't let the water all land in one place, instead he writes out his name across the sheet. The wind blows and he shivers. When the lady came, he waved away the coat she offered. It was hot then, as hot as back in Homs. How could he know then that they would stop here for ever and the wind would arrive bringing wet and snow? And still the lorries don't stop, and the trains whoosh on past to Budapest as though they are frightened of him and Joram. An elephant frightened of an ant. A man frightened of a baby.

No response from the tent. No judder of the canvas from inside. No *rat-a-tat-tat* banging against the plastic to indicate that Aimar should go away since Joram has someone with him, someone Aimar must not see but who he would see later anyway. A man from Libya or Sudan. A man who leaves food which Joram shares with Aimar.

"He go."

Aimar turns. This man is tall and thin and has that Somalian face.

"Soldiers come," the man says. "You not hear?"

Aimar had been shouting through the fence with the others in the morning, before sneaking off to the woods for a shit, his first in two weeks. It had been a good shit, a great long one. He felt lighter, relieved, ready to wander for an hour or so along ditches and through a snicket where he found this bag.

"Everyone go in a bus," the Somali says. "I hide."

Aimar smiles but his smile is a trick. He is not going to fall for any false charm from a man telling him a whopping great tale. Joram wouldn't have gone, not without Aimar.

"Liar." He drops the smile.

"Tell them you're a boy or they put you in a container. No windows." The man from Somalia glances around like this is a foreign place, not somewhere they have waited for a year. "Everyone here is a boy now. You be one too, lad. Maybe then they put you in a house not a camp."

The Somali backs away.

"Where have they taken him?" Aimar calls but the man turns and lopes towards the railway track.

The bag has leaked down the front of Aimar's trousers. He throws it on the mud. His name on the blue plastic sheet has merged into a damp smear, little droplets running out of substance. Around him there is no noise of rustling, no murmurs, no shouting. When Joram was here to call Aimar by his name, he was someone. Now he is alone with the wind, he is nobody.

Stop all the clocks

It's mid-March and Turing appears at the door of the Masters' Common Room in his shirtsleeves, damp marks clearly visible. I am surprised by his arrival.

"Is Mr Eperson here?" he pants. No, *Good evening, Sir*, or *Hello*.

"I believe Mr Eperson will be back shortly," I tell the boy, however I do not share with him that Donald has spent the past half hour with the headmaster discussing the prize that Morcom's mother is intending to establish in her son's name, nor do I inform him that I am lingering here, waiting upon Donald's return.

I glance at the clock, as though I am caught up in some activity, purposefully indicating to Turing that he is not welcome. Yet, the boy does not excuse himself or make any effort to depart.

"Was it something to do with the gramophone society?" I ask concerning Donald's noble effort to show the boys that there are higher considerations than those that normally consume their extracurricular time.

"No," he says and, as usual, he stares boldly at my chest.

If any of the other boys stared so, I would not be disquieted. But with Turing I cross my arms, challenging him to become cognisant of his unsociable gaze and to remedy it by raising his eyes to my face, as any seventeen-year-old surely should be able to.

"You've been running," I say to distract him.

Turing has never been noted as a sportsman, neither here at Sherborne, nor at his previous school. Indeed, he is a boy who has been inclined to watch the daisies grow rather than to pay attention to a game of cricket. Yet recently I have seen him running everywhere, as though to walk is to waste time.

"It helps me think," he says. And then he adds, "And not think."

I find I cannot have any objection to his statement, and yet its boldness irritates me. I wait for him to either explain his presence or leave, but he does neither.

"If it's not concerning the gramophone society," I say, "would it not be more appropriate to seek out your house master?" For really, it is quite impossible for boys to demand masters' time in this way, particularly this wilful, impudent boy who somehow gets away without paying suitable attention to his book work. Except for in Donald's classes, of course, where he appears to be indulged by being set problems that he cannot solve by the light of nature. Donald refers to Turing's solutions to these puzzles as clumsy or cumbersome, judgements which please me for they demonstrate the need for rigorous, disciplined learning. However, to my discontent, Donald very occasionally declares Turing's work to be brilliant.

"I need to speak to Don," he replies.

I clear my throat at the use of a master's Christian name, and a diminutive at that.

"I've been thinking, you see," he continues. "About time and the mind. It's all quite fresh in my head."

He raises his eyes to me for the first time and I see the sadness, and even though I cannot respect this boy with his hopeless obsession with science and mathematics, and his rejection of the classics, I am touched by his situation.

"Perhaps you would like to wait," I say, relenting, and I let him in to the Common Room.

He makes straight for the chess board that Donald has been poring over for the past few days.

"I see you're looking at the game," I say as I clear out my pipe out into the ashtray and unroll my tobacco pouch. "You will be interested to know that it's one played at last month's international chess tournament in San Remo."

I know this from listening to the remarks Donald made as he worked through the game, standing beside him until I detected my presence might have become disconcerting, even no longer welcome, at which point I retreated to the chair in which I now sit. Turing nods and I begin to stuff my pipe, satisfied that in this area, in which he believes himself to be a specialist, I know more than he does.

But then he says, "I believe white wins in twelve moves."

How he can know that by simply looking at the board I do not know. My instinct is to doubt he is correct and to tell him he is being preposterous, speaking well outside his knowledge. I stand, regretting that I invited him in and knowing that, when Donald returns, this boy's presence will prevent any possible mention of the Tchaikovsky recording I recently purchased in the hope that Donald might care to listen to it with me.

"Your tie," I say.

I had not intended commenting on it since I suspected its use was purely to illicit such attention. He glances down to where his tie is threaded round the top of his trousers.

"It is not a belt," I say, reminding him of the purpose of both belt and tie.

"It performs the function of a belt quite adequately," he replies, leaving it where it is.

I hold my lighter to my pipe and suck in the smoke. "Really?" I say as though completely disinterested in the subject, and I pick up a copy of the Iliad, left by some other master, and sit to read.

As Turing leans over the chess board, I cannot help but glance surreptitiously, as I did earlier today with Donald, and I find I am comparing the boy unfavourably with Morcom, who paid diligent attention to neat work and learning, and who never shared Turing's stupid attitude to the sane discussion of the New Testament in my classes. Morcom's interest in the chess game would not have seen him slouching so over the board, and I find that I am deeply regretting the loss of the boy destined to take up a scholarship at Cambridge. I turn a page in the book.

And then Turing is up, pacing the room in a manner that makes it impossible for me to pretend to ignore him.

"If one could travel at the speed of light," he says, "then one would never appear to age to a static observer." He pauses. "In non-accelerating conditions, of course."

The speed of light? Non-accelerating? What is this boy talking about?

"Time would appear to stand still for the observed, stop all together. Do you think that is what death is?"

"There is one place you will find the answer, Turing," I say, referring to the Bible, as I do so often in class.

"But then, as Einstein said, travelling at the speed of light is impossible, so it can't be."

The arrogance of the child to presume to comment on such matters.

"What I want to ask Don is whether he thinks Chris might have moved to a frame of reference where he is travelling at almost the speed of light relative to ours," he persists, "so that for us observers, Chris will barely age over the duration of our lifetimes."

I stand and tap my pipe on the edge of the fireplace while I think how to stop this nonsense.

"I long to understand what has become of him," he says.

That much is apparent.

"Christopher Morcom died of bovine tuberculosis," I answer bluntly.

"Yes," Turing replies. "But what has become of his mind? You see, there is still work for us to do together. I must not let him down now I am left to do it alone. I feel sure we will meet again somewhere and I will need to account to him."

I do not know how to reply to this. The obsession Turing had for Morcom in life – sharing books with him in the library; passing notes unashamedly in class; staring quite unabashed at him during the gramophone society meetings, according to the giggling of the other boys - seems to have taken a queer route now Morcom is dead.

"We cannot tell why Morcom should have suffered such a death." I retreat to the safety of the lines the boys were told a month ago. "But there must have been a reason. Maybe to save him from pain and illness, or maybe to help you boys in some way, for a friend can often, by his death, do more to influence others than even in his life."

"Exactly," Turing says and for a moment I think I might have made myself understood by this boy for once. "But I would like to know what has become of his mind. You see, if the mind could be considered to be a series of logical thoughts, perhaps Chris might in some way live on."

The idea is ludicrous. I suspect the leniency accorded to Turing by some of the staff has allowed his brain to overheat.

"More prayer," I state.

"I have this idea that the mind's processes could be captured in some way; that simple mental operations might be performed in a mind machine. Maybe even perform the complex task of playing chess." He waves towards the board. "I should very much like to have been able to discuss this with Chris. I shall not find anywhere a companion so brilliant and yet so charming and unconceited."

Turing's constant references to Morcom have become grating, alarming even. Then he adds, "Have you ever had a friend like Chris?"

I turn to the fire place to tap my pipe and avoid his gaze. Even though this boy is seventeen-years-old, he speaks in the unguarded way of a child. Unwordly, and yet his innocence is confusingly beguiling.

"Morcom is dead." I know I say this harshly. I pull my shoulders back and turn to face him as any master should be able to with a boy. "To go on like this serves no purpose, Turing. None at all."

For a moment he smiles, then I realise that it is not a smile at all. His mouth and eyes tighten as though about to cry, and as I attempt to check any possible tears by clearing my throat, the clock chimes half past.

"See," I say, demonstrating that time ticks regularly and eternally on.

But with the passing of another half hour, I wonder whether Donald might not have headed straight back to his lodgings, whether I have waited here in vain.

"I worshiped the ground he walked on," he adds.

"Enough," I say. "You must put a stop to this, to these unnatural passions right now."

"Excuse me, Sir," Turing says. "I didn't mean to upset you."

And as I turn back to the fire, I hear the study door open and the click of his heels in the corridor hastening as he reaches the main door where he sets off running, running, always running.

The Sundance Kid

There were two police cars outside our house. The second I saw them, my chest clutched my breaths. The police had parked like that, two cars right outside our house, the time we'd been burgled, when the kitchen window was smashed – all glass and blood in the sink – and the TV gone, and Mum's ring, the one her grandmother left her, taken. And they had been in my bedroom and thrown my pyjamas on the floor, tipped up my mattress and taken the *iPad* Dad had given me for two birthdays and a Christmas. And my Chelsea bag. Mum had cried about my Chelsea bag. It wouldn't be worth replacing my *iPad*, Dad had said on the phone, they might come back.

I sprinted to my house when I saw those two cars, my school bag whacking against my back. I beat on the door: *Mum, Mum.* She opened it, big and real. Except –

"What have they taken?" I panted.

She looked through me, not at me, like I wasn't there at all.

"Mum?" I could hardly say her name. My jaw had locked shut.

"You're moving into my room." Mum's face didn't move, like she wasn't Mum anymore, like she was someone else wearing Mum's body and Mum's clothes. "Joe and Alison are having yours."

"Wha?"

Joe only lived next door. It didn't make sense that he and his mum were staying with us.

"Just tonight," the other person who'd taken over Mum's body said.

It had been OK sleeping in with Mum after the burglary, until she'd redecorated my room and my toys were cleaned as good as new, like no one had ever been anywhere near them. I was older now though.

"Hurry up." She pulled my bag from my shoulder. "They're on their way over."

I didn't want to move my stuff into Mum's room or sleep with her in her bed.

"Now!"

Joe's parents were as old as everyone else's grandparents. Joe was a late arrival, Mum said. Not a mistake, just unexpected. He had a cowboy hut in his garden, which his dad had built for his sixth birthday. A wood shed with shelves and a wooden cowboy bunk. Outside, a cowboy, taller even than his dad, leant back against the hut, his hat tipped down over his eyes, hands in his pockets, legs crossed at the ankles. His dad had carved the cowboy out of a tree trunk, painted it black, called him The Sundance Kid. He'd given Joe a cowboy hat and a cap gun, and Joe had a cowboy birthday party where we lassoed a bucket of sweets, just like proper cowboys. We'd baked beans in that hut, prepared cow hides, spat tobacco into a spittoon.

No one else had a cowboy hut like Joe's. No one else had a Sundance Kid.

Joe and Alison turned up with a policewoman. Mum talked about cups of tea with sugar. I ate three *Jaffa Cakes* without her noticing and my eye started blinking without me wanting it to, just like it used to.

Joe stood by the kitchen door, hands in his pockets, head down like The Sundance Kid's. His mum didn't say a word.

"Why don't you take Joe up?" Mum said, all sing-song.

I nodded and waited for someone to tell me that Joe's house had been burgled, that the rooms had all been turned upside down, that human shit had been smeared on their walls and someone had pissed on their carpets. No one did.

"OK," I said.

Joe followed me upstairs to my room where we played *Minecraft* for a million hours. Downstairs, teaspoons clinked and more policemen arrived and muttered away.

"Did they take a lot?" I asked.

Joe raised his head. His lips were the same colour as his face, his eyes focussed past me like Mum's had.

"I think Dad's dead," he said.

"What?" I said like I hadn't heard properly, like I was stupid.

"I think –" Joe didn't finish, he left it at that.

114

"Shit," I said, because we fought Indians together, we skidded our bikes till our tyres wore down to the fabric, we herded cattle. No one died.

"When can I have my room back?"

They had spent a whole week sleeping in my room and watching our TV, and they still weren't gone. We were waiting for the inquest, Mum said. Alison didn't feel comfortable returning to the house until everything was settled. She didn't like the thought of that at all.

No one at school said anything to Joe. They didn't say much to me either. Whatever Joe had done, I had done too because Joe was living with me. And anyway, I was sleeping with my mum.

Mum said it was the least neighbours could do, after all, no one would wish what they were going through on their worst enemy. She bought more biscuits.

Joe had to be a witness at the inquest because he had discovered the body. His mum had gone off to work and he had made his dad a cup of coffee. He called and called and then gone to look. His dad was hanging there, rope lassoed round The Sundance Kid's hat. The cowboy took Joe's dad's weight. It was well made, they said, sturdy. Joe had left the coffee by his dad's feet.

The letter said that Joe had been the best thing his dad had ever done. It said he loved Alison, that she was the love of his life, always had been, always would be. It said he wanted her to be happy and this way, with him out of the equation, she was free to follow her heart.

I moved back into my room with Joe when Alison went to live with Dave. Joe said he didn't want to go to anywhere near Dave or his house. Alison cried leaving him, all red eyes and snot and tears. Mum said to give it time, to let water flow under the bridge and anyway, it would probably be OK for a short while. Joe and I got along, didn't we?

I didn't mind Joe living with us; I had got used to him. I wanted to tell him he could share my dad, but my dad wasn't like Joe's dad. My dad never made me a cowboy hut, never organised a birthday party. My dad never sang me to sleep.

Lucky Underpants

We stand up and kiss, and then we sit down and kiss, and before long we're lying on the half circle rug. She is above me and her tongue slips into my mouth and I am ever so grateful. This is going to be fantastic, me and Rebecca on the rug. God, this is the best.

Then I hear her toe tapping on the floorboard. For a moment I try to ignore the regular tap-tapping before I realise that the rhythm syncopates with the movement of her mouth and I cannot help but think of gnawing. And then I am thinking animals, a moose chewing cud in particular. And then I'm wondering why I'm thinking of a moose, and anyway, does a moose even chew cud? Just as I'm about to pull my head away from the pressure of her lips she twists off me and sits. I can't help checking her feet, the boot sole that must have been responsible for the tapping.

"Don't you want to?" she asks, and all I can think of is, "How many stomachs does a cow have?"

The room's dead silent. I itch my chin against her shoulder and realise I'm no closer to finding out whether my lucky underpants have been successful or not.

"I think it's five," I say.

Rebecca tucks in her blouse.

"Nothing happened," she says. "Remember that. Nothing happened."

"No one has any intention of building a wall."

(Walter Ulbricht, Head of the German Democratic Republic (DDR), 14th June 1961)

It's 5.30pm on Saturday 12th August 1961 and Gabi Liebknecht is standing outside her grandmother's apartment in Bernauer Strasse, Berlin, leaning against the pockmarked wall. Casually, she glances at the house opposite where Peter lives. Peter is fifteen and has blonde hair and blue eyes. Two days ago he stopped to ask her name. She hasn't seen him since and now she thinks he must be out.

Click, clack, round the corner come two French soldiers, guns over their shoulders, *click, clack, click, clack.* Gabi rests a foot behind her on the wall. One of the soldiers slows as he approaches.

"Gabi," her grandmother calls down from the window. "Come and help."

The soldier smiles down at Gabi and says something. Gabi doesn't speak French.

"Now, Gabi."

"Coming, Oma," Gabi calls.

The soldier repeats what he's said, all the words running into one like a waterfall. She smiles back.

"Now, Gabi," Gabi mimics.

The soldier laughs and rests his hand briefly on her shoulder, before striding off to catch up with his colleague. She watches the pair turn into Ruppiner Strasse, the heat of his palm still on her skin.

Gabi is fourteen, too old to be sent to stay with her grandmother while her parents visit her father's aunt in Hanover, but she knows she isn't here for her own sake. Oma is lonely and her memory isn't what it used to be, and then there's her hip. And anyway, Gabi has always spent time here during the summer holidays when the rest of her friends head off to the Wannsee or across to West Germany to visit relatives. Why change now?

Running her fingers over the bullet holes, Gabi saunters to the door of 48 Bernauer Strasse and, as she steps from the pavement into the lobby, she leaves the French sector of Berlin and enters the Soviet sector. Sixteen years ago someone, somewhere decreed that the front wall of Gabi's grandmother's block of apartments should constitute the boundary between the two zones, leaving the inhabitants living in East Berlin, but their only entrance and exit in the west.

"*Guten Tag.*" Ida Siekmann's door on the first-floor shoots open, as though she has been waiting all afternoon to hear footsteps. "Are you staying with your grandmother again?"

"Yes, Frau Siekmann," Gabi replies. "Just for two weeks." Then she adds, "Mutti and Vati are in Hanover."

"Hanover." Ida Seikmann nods her head.

Frau Seikmann hasn't been here long. She moved from Gorki, Poland, to be near her sister a couple of blocks away in French administered Wedding. Oma repeats this news to Gabi often, except Oma still calls Gorki Gorken and says it's in West Prussia.

"Why do they have to mess around with countries?" Oma says a lot. Gabi has given up commenting.

Having repeated Hanover, Frau Siekmann waits. She has no one other than her sister, Oma says, not since the war, and never anything to say.

Inside the Siekmann apartment Gabi spies a hat on a chair and the plastic handbag that all women in East Berlin carry, marking them out when they come over to the west of the city. And she has the same cream sofa and wooden table and cream TV that everyone in the DDR has, not Oma though, who still has her furniture from before the war.

"How's school?" Ida Siekmann asks.

Gabi watches the wrinkles in Frau Siekmann's face open and close as she speaks and she wonders how old she is. Sixty perhaps.

"Good, thank you," Gabi answers. "It's the holiday now."

"Ah, yes."

Frau Siekmann's hand fiddles with her door latch.

"Oma called me in."

As though relieved that an end to the conversation has been found, Frau Siekmann steps back inside her flat. "You'd better go then," she says.

"Good evening, Frau Siekmann." Gabi waves as she runs on up the stairs.

In the kitchen, Frau Schmidt, from the ground floor, is sitting at the table. Oma is shaking her head as a pan of potatoes bubbles away.

"Frau Schmidt has come to tell us that Doctor Brecht has left," she says.

Frau Schmidt talks to Oma like this all the time now. The dentist has left, fields of corn out in the countryside lie unharvested because the framers have left, there's no one to teach the children. Everyone is leaving for the West. Frau Schmidt's world is full of this talk.

"Who's going to look after my Hans now?" Frau Schmidt says.

Hans Schmidt was only four years old when he was shot in the face by the advancing Soviet troops in May '45. He has one eye and repeated infections in the remaining empty socket.

"They won't leave us with no doctors," Oma says. She believes this.

"Twelve and a half thousand East Germans have left for the west this week alone," Frau Schmidt says.

The borders that stem the flow of emigrants between East and West Germany elsewhere don't work in Berlin where Berliners, East and West, criss-cross the city every day for work. Berlin is a loophole where East Germans can travel to make day visits to relatives in West Berlin, carrying only a small bag of belongings to show they have every intention of returning home. And with that small bag they start their new lives in the west. Vast transit camps have been set up in West Berlin to gather together the skilled and educated emigrants. And all this is possible because the victorious Second World War allies divided the country's capital city, now located deep within the DDR, into four, in preference to letting it fall into the hands of the Soviets.

"He could see Doctor Litfin." Gabi suggests her own family doctor in an attempt to stall Frau Schmidt's gathering rant.

"He could see Doctor Litfin," Oma repeats.

"If we can travel down to Kreuzberg," Frau Schmidt replies.

Gabi stabs a potato to see if it's cooked. This sort of talk really irritates Gabi now she's fourteen and knows a bit about the world. Who's going to stop Frau Schmidt taking the one-eyed Hans to see Doctor Litfin five kilometres away in American-administered Kreuzberg?

"I hear that today border guards are stopping trains coming into Berlin and interrogating passengers." Frau Schmidt shakes her head. "Most are being sent back to where they came from."

"No one will stop us travelling around in Berlin," Gabi says, banging the pan in the sink as she drains the water. "The Americans won't allow it."

The Americans, British and French didn't let the Soviets starve them out in 1948, and now they maintain secure transport links between West Berlin and the rest of West Germany. The Americans will look after them. Oma nods.

"Maybe the Americans don't care about us anymore." Frau Schmidt crosses her arms.

"Doctor Litfin might travel here to see Doctor Brecht's patients," Gabi says, steering the conversation away from Frau Schmidt's speculation.

"A doctor visit Soviet Berlin when he's free!" Frau Schmidt laughs.

"They won't leave us without doctors," Oma says again.

Gabi sets out the knives and forks for the evening meal, brushing against Frau Schmidt's arm to show her she's in the way. Frau Schmidt takes the hint.

"I better get back to my Hans," she says.

Only once she's gone, does Gabi ask, "Will Mutti and Vati be all right getting back from Hanover?"

"Why couldn't those people leave our country as it was?" Oma replies and Gabi wishes she hadn't said anything.

As Gabi piles potatoes onto the plates, Oma puts an arm round her waist and, for a brief moment, Gabi lets her cheek rest on her grandmother's crinkly hair. But the hair prickles and she pulls away to add a wurst to each of the plates.

Later, in her bedroom, Gabi rubs her soap-dry hands and looks down into hot Bernauer Strasse, hoping to catch sight of Peter. She can't wait to get back home and tell her friends about him. She's not tired and yet it's bedtime, so she lies down on top of her eiderdown and splays her hair out over the pillow to cool. Dull, dull, dull. She counts the remaining days.

Gabi thinks she must have overslept for all the commotion going on outside in the street, talking, shouting, running. The curtains are glowing dim. It feels far too early for such movement. And then she remembers it's Sunday in any case. From the kitchen she hears Frau Schmidt's voice. She steps out of bed.

"Is that a risk you're prepared to take?" Frau Schmidt is saying.

They are drinking coffee, Frau Schmidt and Oma, in Oma's kitchen. Gabi rubs her face. Can it really be late enough for Frau Schmidt to be visiting?

"What's the time?" she asks, blinking the blur from her eyes.

"I'm staying put." Oma tops up the coffee.

Gabi focuses on the clock. It's five past seven. There's a rap at the door, sharp enough to make the women start.

"Shall I open the door?" Gabi asks.

"More fool you," Frau Schmidt says.

At the door stands Hans, his one eye staring at Gabi. Gabi has never liked Hans. He has always known what he wanted and, because of his one eye, has always been given it. Last year, in the stairwell, he shoved her into the corner, his hot body heavy against hers and he had grabbed at her breasts, put his hand up her skirt, rooted around until she had wriggled a hand free and poked him in that empty eye socket, made it bleed, reawakened a latent infection. This year she stands well back to let him pass. He doesn't dawdle.

"I've been all the way up Schwedter Strasse," he reports. "And along Garten Strasse. There's barbed wire and border guards everywhere. All crossings are closed. The Brandenburg Gate is closed. Everyone's saying the barbed wire is temporary," he pauses. "They're going to build a wall."

"Oh my god, it's true!" Frau Schmidt shrieks and grabs her one-eyed son. "Thank God you're safe."

"The Westies are gathering on the other side, shouting at the guards," Hans continues.

"The Westies!" Oma claps her hand down on the table. "There are no Westies or Easties. We are all Berliners. This city cannot be divided by barbed wire or a wall or anything. The Americans will not allow it."

"Just look out at the street, Oma," Hans says, hands in pockets, his good eye rolling up in its socket. Gabi wants to shove her sharp nails into that empty space all over again.

"We're going home to pack," Frau Schmidt says.

"It'll be back to normal tomorrow," Oma says.

"You're deluded," Frau Schmidt says.

And Frau Schmidt and Hans are off, down the stairs, into their apartment to pack a suitcase or two, before stepping out of 48 Bernauer Strasse onto the free, French pavement in West Berlin while their front door still allows.

"Shall we go, Oma?" Gabi asks.

"Your mother was born in this apartment," Oma replies. "And here," she pats the table, "this is where I heard the news that your Opa had been crushed to death in Luisen Strasse, searching for food for his family while those bastards bombed the life out of us."

"What if Frau Schmidt's right?"

"Your parents will be back next week," Oma says. "Then you will go home."

It's early morning on Tuesday 22nd August 1961 and Gabi Lieb-knecht's grandmother is still asleep. Nothing more has been heard from Frau Schmidt and Hans, or the fifty other households in Bernauer Strasse who took the opportunity to flee. A number of East German border guards, one of whom features prominently in foreign newspapers, jumping with his rifle over coiled barbed wire, have also escaped. The U-Bahn trains, which ten days earlier linked West to East to West, no longer stop at Bernauer Strasse underground station, or any other station in East Berlin. Instead they clatter through the dimly lit, well-guarded, ghost stations on their route between the French north and American south. The flow of Germans from the DDR has slowed from a deluge to a faltering trickle, just like that, overnight.

Over the past four days the East German authorities have been making slow progress up Bernauer Strasse, bricking in the doors and windows on the south side of the street which once gave direct access to the west. Today, they have arrived at 48 Bernauer Strasse with their bricks and mortar. Already there is no front door. The exit to the building is now a temporary opening bashed in at the back, securely located in the Soviet administered sector.

Until today, Gabi's grandmother has stood firm. They have heard nothing from Gabi's parents and have no idea whether they have been able to return from Hanover, so Gabi has remained. In any case, if there really is to be no possibility of travel between the two halves of the city, who will look after the old, failing woman if Gabi goes?

Outside, on the north of Bernauer Strasse, Gabi sees Peter leaving his front door, off to meet up with friends, perhaps, or to listen to Elvis. She waves at him and he hesitates before crossing the street. She opens the window.

"Why are you still there?" he calls up to her.

"I'm taking care of Oma," she replies and to her, her words called down to the blonde-haired Peter, sound not just practical but romantic.

"You are mad to stay so long. You must leave, today. Look!"

Gabi knows that the bottom floor of their building is already bricked up and that the guards are now moving up to Frau Siekmann's apartment on the first floor.

"I will talk to Oma," she says.

"Don't talk," Peter replies. "Tell her."

Gabi smiles and nods, and then Peter does something which angers her.

"You're bloody stupid," he shouts and as he turns away the ridiculousness of her romantic notions hit her.

Without waking her grandmother, she packs her few things. All is not yet lost. Each day so far the West Berlin fire brigade have been in Bernauer Strasse, holding out jumping sheets for people escaping from higher rooms. There is no longer any doubt in her mind that she will be waiting for them when they turn up shortly, as they surely will.

There's a knock at the front door. Gabi hesitates, fearing that the guards have already come to move them away from the apartment further into Soviet territory. She curses herself for her idiocy in staying so long.

"It's Frau Siekmann," a woman's voice whispers. "Ida."

For a moment Gabi isn't sure. Perhaps Frau Siekmann has been put up to this by the guards to trick Gabi into opening.

"Please let me in," Frau Siekmann says.

Gabi opens the door a crack, peers through it at the landing and, seeing only Frau Siekmann, lets her slip in.

"They are in my apartment," Ida Siekmann tells her.

Gabi's heart pounds, her throat tightens. "The fire brigade will be here shortly," she says. "We'll jump."

Frau Siekmann passes her plastic handbag from one hand to the other, a very small bag, the one she would have carried with her on a visit to her sister's two weeks ago, nothing much in it at all. Her eyes dart, her mouth opens and closes, taking tiny little clips of air.

"I must go to my sister," she says.

From downstairs Gabi hears guards' boots pounding.

"In the front," she says, pointing to her room while she hurries to deal with her grandmother.

The news later that day, reported by the international press gathered in Bernauer Strasse, tells of Ida Siekmann dropping an eiderdown onto the pavement, followed by a few possessions, and then, before the firemen were able to open their jumping sheet, she threw herself out. Nothing much is known about her, except that now Ida Siekmann, who died on her way to the hospital, is the first casualty of the wall.

Back up on the second floor, Gabi first hears yells from the street. She looks out and recognises the flowers on her eiderdown. Her grandmother stirs. Gabi looks from Oma to the small ring of people fussing over a pile of clothes down below. She has strong bones and a strong mind. Oma has neither. Downstairs, boots crunch and trowels scrape cement. She waves at the firemen.

"Here," she calls. "Here."

And as they gather beneath her grandmother's bedroom window, Gabi grabs a photo of Oma, Opa and Mutti. She grabs her grandmother's comb, because it comes readily to hand, and a cushion that Mutti embroidered as a child.

"Oma," she says, shaking the precious woman awake. "We're leaving."

"I'm not ..."

"Now," Gabi says and she throws the handful of her grandmother's belongings down onto the jumping sheet, followed by her own small case. "It's not hard. See."

Her grandmother shakes her head. Gabi leads her to the window.

"You go first, Oma. I'll follow."

"I'm not leaving."

"You must." Gabi blinks and swallows. "There's no life for us two here. We need to be with Mutti and Vati. They'll look after us. We can't be here alone."

And as she sits on the window ledge, legs dangling outside, words of encouragement are shouted up from the street.

"Take my hand, Oma. Sit with me, here. Just sit. That's it. Now swing your legs round. Please, Oma. There, that's it. Hear what they're saying? Push outwards, shuffle your bottom forward and push off outwards. Hear them, Oma? Please don't cry. We'll be OK." Gabi smiles. "There," she says, pointing. "I think it's Mutti. There. See. She's waving at us. We must go to her, Oma. Do it now, I'll follow. Everything will be all right."

About the Author

Ruth Brandt enjoys exploring settings in her short stories, what they suggest to her about the inhabitants and the divisions they create – political, familial and the resulting intrapersonal conflicts.

Ruth has an MFA in Creative Writing from Kingston University where she won the MFA Creative Writing Prize 2016. She has been published by Aesthetica, Litro, Neon Magazine, Bridport Prize Anthology and many more, and was nominated for the Pushcart Prize and the Write Well Award in 2016, and Best Small Fictions 2019. She teaches creative writing, including at West Dean College, and was formerly Writer in Residence at the Surrey Wildlife Trust and the National Trust's Polesden Lacey.

She lives in Surrey with her hugely supportive husband and has two delightful sons.

About Fly on the Wall Press

A publisher with a conscience.
Publishing high quality anthologies on pressing issues,
chapbooks and poetry products, from exceptional poets around the globe.
Founded in 2018 by founding editor, Isabelle Kenyon.

Other publications:

Please Hear What I'm Not Saying

Persona Non Grata

Bad Mommy / Stay Mommy by Elisabeth Horan

The Woman With An Owl Tattoo by Anne Walsh Donnelly

the sea refuses no river by Bethany Rivers

White Light White Peak by Simon Corble

Second Life by Karl Tearney

The Dogs of Humanity by Colin Dardis

Small Press Publishing: The Dos and Don'ts by Isabelle Kenyon

Alcoholic Betty by Elisabeth Horan

Awakening by Sam Love

Grenade Genie by Tom McColl

House of Weeds by Amy Kean and Jack Wallington

No Home In This World by Kevin Crowe

The Goddess of Macau by Graeme Hall

The Prettyboys of Gangster Town by Martin Grey

The Sound of the Earth Singing to Herself by Ricky Ray

Inherent by Lucia Orellana Damacela

Medusa Retold by Sarah Wallis

Pigskin by David Hartley

We Are All Somebody

Aftereffects by Jiye Lee

Someone Is Missing Me by Tina Tamsho-Thomas

Odd as F*ck by Anne Walsh Donnelly

Muscle and Mouth by Louise Finnigan

Modern Medicine by Lucy Hurst

These Mothers of Gods by Rachel Bower

Andy and the Octopuses by Isabelle Kenyon

Sin Is Due To Open In A Room Above Kitty's by Morag Anderson

Fauna by Dr. David Hartley

How To Bring Him Back by Claire HM

History of Forgetfulness by Shahe Mankerian

Social Media:

@fly_press (Twitter)

@flyonthewall_poetry (Instagram)

@flyonthewallpress (Facebook)

www.flyonthewallpress.co.uk